CATHERINE, CATHERINE

Catherine, Catherine

LESBIAN SHORT STORIES

by

Ingrid MacDonald

women's
PRESS

The author would like to acknowledge her reliance on historical research and the translation of trial documents in the case of Catherina Margaretha Linck (1721), undertaken by Brigitte Eriksson and published as "A Lesbian Execution In Germany" in *The Journal of Homosexuality*. The author would also like to thank the Banff Centre for the Arts and the participants of the May Studios, 1991; the women of Aristazabal — Lina Chartrand, Liz Ukrainetz and Jennifer Rudder; Helen Humphreys; Mary Louise Adams; and Ann Decter for encouraging this book into being. The manuscript was produced with the support of the City of Toronto through the Toronto Arts Council.

"Travelling West" was previously published in *Prism International*; "Catherine, Catherine" in *Dykewords* (Women's Press); "Want for Nothing" was published as "Upstairs there is a room with a bed" in *More Serious Pleasure* (Sheba Feminist Publishers, Cleis Press).

CANADIAN CATALOGUING IN PUBLICATION DATA
MacDonald, Ingrid
    Catherine, Catherine

ISBN 0-88961-164-5
1. Lesbians - Fiction. 2. Linck, Catherina. 3. Lesbians - Prussia (Germany)
- History. I. Title.
PS8575.D65C3 1991   C813'.54   C91-095101-2
PR9199.3.M33C3 1991

Published by Women's Press, 517 College Street, Suite 233,
Toronto, Ontario, Canada M6G 4A2

Cover art: Jody Hewgill
Cover design: Joanne Claus and Christine Higdon
Copy editing and proofreading: Ellen Quigley

Women's Press gratefully acknowledges financial support from The Canada Council and the Ontario Arts Council.
Printed and bound in Canada.   2 3 4 5 1995 1994

for Rita

CONTENTS

❋ ❋ ❋

Overwintering

WINTER

*

To the corner store. Out of the car, 15 below freezing, too cold to snow. In my mitts the money that buys the milk — just before the store closes. Mr. Hoy dampers the snow that's caught in the sway of the blue canvass and rolls the stiff awning up for the night. Mrs. Hoy doesn't look when she gives three pennies change. She is almost closed.

Stores and houses have trees full of light, but it's as cold as Jupiter out here. Blue snow crunches under my feet. Nobody on the streets, no notebook, no point of reference, nothing to measure. A jumpstart engine turning over and halting. Steaming rows of chimneystacks. Ice coating the fences around the loading docks for the eastbound grain.

Fieldnotes describe the earth, the earth muttering, trying to tell me something.

In my parka, my body is warm but feels cold. I am a mass of warm air dissipating, my particles bevey and swell into all the holes of the night. Tingling hands, numb feet, sensation lost. The electric field of cold night takes me into herself particle by particle. I lose all the marking points. I stop the car, breath cold inside, outside the putterings of white exhaust. *Tu-vita-vit, tu-vita-tu-vita, vita, vita.* Lonely song of a winter owl. Hurry up and come, my life to me.

*

I've drifted again, like snow.

Athena's Palace Greek restaurant. Bowls of black olives, tzatziki, baskets of pita bread sopped with olive oil, blue and white chequered table cloths. Lina's snapping her fingers in front of my face. "Earth to Hilary."

I come back, surprised. "Just keeping those hemispheres open for an Aha! experience," I say.

"Like what used to happen in bed," Lina says, kidding, but I hear hurt whistling like wind through a window not quite closed.

"Don't make jokes about that."

"Forget it then."

It's not the right time to open anything up, but this discomfort between us seems so obvious, a wound opened. "Maybe we should see someone ..."

She stiffens. "What could they do?"

It's her birthday. Here's her birthday present. I've framed a photo of her and me, taken when we were first in love. It's the only picture that exists of us as a couple. Taken in the field, we're on the Pacific, on the northwest side of Vancouver Island. I'm finishing my graduate thesis on the relationship between urchins and kale and the habitats of the otter. It's a more delicate relationship than you'd imagine, between the urchins and the kale.

More food arrives. I touch her leg affectionately, hold her hand under the table cloth. The waiter brings more and more food, and soon the table is covered in plates. We've over-ordered. Lina looks at the picture of me and says, "You're beautiful." What would we tell someone? That love used to saturate us. Like two fish brilliant and opalescent in ethyl alcohol. Love gave us bright round eyes, floated our hair like feathery fins. Ethyl alcohol evaporates. Every ichthyologist soon learns, if you don't top off the jars regularly, you get wrinkly fish.

I look in her face, round with strong features, like the moon, under a mane of thick black hair. The echo of her telling me I'm beautiful hangs in the air. She has barely eaten. I look down at my hands, solid as two fish in my lap. I want to break the circle of this silence, but I have nothing to say.

I eat what I can, but it is not enough.

*

We go to Lavender Lanes' AIDS fundraiser. It's bitterly cold and crystal clear tonight, but all our friends are here. Philomina and Jan in lane five, Betty and Lou-Lou in six, Marika and Jody in seven and us in eight. Betty and Lou-Lou bought a triple-decker cake, green and pink roses. The Lanes dim the incandescents when Betty lights the candles.

I don't budge from the bench all night. Lina bowls my turns for me. Tallying up our scores she says, "I'm keeping you alive."

I almost say how preposterous that is, but I look at the other couples. Ebullience and laughter. Marika doubled over, pointing at Jody's guttered ball. Tears on Lou-Lou's face from laughing.

13

Nobody seems to have the same problems as us. When we try to talk, when we try to make love, when we try to spend time together, we get to a point and then stop.

Everything that is hard for us has been accumulating since fall.

At night in bed when Lina would touch me I would feel the folds of a heavy curtain, pulled against who I am, who we are. "No, don't," I would say, putting her hand away. It hurts less this way. We turn back. In the mornings, I lie in bed with dread pouring over me, an ocean of dread breaking against me, lapping over me. While the radio plays in the kitchen, Lina comes in, dressed to go. "I'm off to the market then."

"Sleep well?" I ask, though I slept beside her. No memory of night.

"I slept okay," non-committal answer, her face haggard and rough, like she's been crying. She wouldn't tell me, if she had. Keeps things to herself. Get up you lazy girl. To Lina I say, "What?"

"I didn't say anything," she says, going out the door.

Lina blows out the birthday candles. The lights come back on, and the clatter of bowling pins resume. I say, "I must be overwintering." My head is down; I'm crumbling bits of cake for a path of ants to carry off. Overwintering is what Lina does to make the garden ready for the snow. She turns the compost for the last time, cuts back the raspberries, buries the tulip bulbs, brings the sensitive ones inside, gets the whole project ready to be dead for a couple of months.

"Are you ever overwintering," she says and walks away to talk with the others. I see her having fun with them, pointing at score cards and slapping Jean on the ass, but she glances back at me, with trouble in her eyes. I hear *Tu-vita-vit*.

Overwintering

I see my lover's face turning away.

*

Carrying the milk and three pennies, I come in through the garage, stamp the snow off my boots.

In the kitchen, I stand on the mat of our quiet house, everything clean and in its place, the dishes dried and put away, a single light burning. I hear the smallest sound. I've left it too late. The smallest sound. The sound of the light switching off in Lina's bedroom. Her apron hangs on its hook, and I press my face against it, feel it, a dry hush of uncried tears against yellow flowers fading. They've been her yellow flowers since she was little, since she was my age, the age of holding three pennies and wishing Jupiter would go away.

SPRING

* *

The smallest birds are jewels in the crown of a tree. A rufous hummingbird small and agile, her wingspan fits like a flower inside an opened mouth. Sweet nectar sucked through a needle-shaped bill. Wings blurring, frontwards, backwards in flight. Nature is the earth's most perfect clock, and my tiny birds have arrived exactly on time, flying flower to flower to their nests. Nests are like fields, containing the whole world briefly. Like wombs they are round.

There's a nest here in the lower bough of this cedar, barely bigger than a thimble. Made of lichen, plant down, spider silk, moss and slivers of bark. I am here quietly breathing, hidden under branches and falling upwards into a universe only as big as two birds and their eggs. Two eggs the size of jelly beans hold hummingbirds of the future, called forth by *chip-churp-churp* of their parents.

Knowing the world through this field, feeling it, living it, like a dream lived, awake. My body is brittle and not ready to dream you yet. I'm only ready to be on this island with you, and this green island belongs to us, because we honour it, because we study how it is tied together by moss and rust tinted soil and giant sitka trees and animals and plants. I cannot give myself to you, though in shame and in secrecy I wish to. I give myself to this island, to the hummingbirds.

* *

Overwintering

Lina on the radio-phone, by the kitchen at camp. Passing boats scatter squall on the line, interjecting codes, building a curtain of resistance. I feel broken. Through fragments — how are? what's it? are you? — I try to open, try to glue the bits of talk together into some sense of how we used to be. Static and distance crackles. We're shouting and the words bounce back from the radio-phone into my lap. We get part way in, the line surges. "It's too damn hard. I'll try on the weekend," I say and we are closed, like a store full of things we need, milk and comfort items, stacked up behind the glass window.

* *

At dusk, alone by the lake, a single tree lush and luminescent against a violet, turquoise sky. A train of clouds out on the sea. Thick cold strong wind. "This is my body," I say to the sea, "This is my body," I say to myself.

It is my body, and I can live in it as I please. I know this, but I've given it away to Lina. I cry until all the colours of the sky pour into me, and I am luminescent and weak. How am I ever going to ask for my body back?

* *

You find me. On my back, my legs sticking out under the tree. Quietly, not to disturb anything, you hold your hands out to me. Fingers are bulky and warm, drawing all of me out, pulling me with arms. I find myself hugging you, smelling your smell, in an unspoken moment, unlikely and right. "Come," you say.

I take your hand and we walk to lunch, as two friends would. Innocence in your cool dry hand while mine burns like a touched thistle. I take my hand away and look at it, at its contradiction. Beautiful and undisturbed and intact my hand opens to me like an eye. A pulse describes my body to my heart.

* *

My body feels awakened, but full of ghosts, memories. The party, the kind-of-wedding Lina and I had when we decided to live together. Even my parents came, bravely smiling and shaking hands with interest. Lina was a little late, me waiting at home with my mother and father and some of our friends. Lina stuck in traffic on a Saturday afternoon, behind a Shriners' parade, cursing the patriarchy, in a purple pant suit, leaning on the horn. My mother threw confetti and told me I looked like her mother did on her wedding day. That was a nice thing to say, especially because I was wearing a black dress.

* *

Lina's letter: I'll send you something in the next drop. What do you want? Good coffee? Bagels? Marmalade? Do you need anything? Shampoo? Cream rinse? Tampons? Let me know.

* *

I want : seeds that take a long time to grow.
          : a picket fence. A solid boundary that describes where
I begin, where I end.
          : to be a lover. (Whose?)
          : to tell somebody something. (Not sure what.)

* *

18

Overwintering

I don't want any things. Not things. Things don't hold the world in place. Things don't fix anything. All the things of the world are only floating on a sea that the heart makes. I seem to have a faulty heart. It migrates like a hummingbird searching for its nest. It swims upstream like a salmon, to the river of its birth.

* *

Something deep in me shifting, fleeting, flying flower to flower, moving so fast it gets blurry wings. To desire means to live under the stars, to live by the stars. I look at my hands; they are such beautiful hands. My body feels solid and warm. When I think of you, I think of your breath. I see it leaving you and filling the air, for me to inhale.

* *

I could go to the antarctic and study penguins.
   Do I even like penguins?

* *

We finish lunch with coffee from a thermos and then I station myself under the hummingbird tree. From there I study the nest, the slightest crack showing on one of the eggs. I have three more days before they'll be born. *Chup-chup*, the hummingbird calls. The river is cold from the runoff, but you go there and as if I have never seen a woman before, as if I am not one myself, I watch you. Beauty feels new to me. I have forgotten it in myself for so long I doubted its purpose, but I see it in you. You draw a basin of water from the river and carefully fold your shirt on a rock in the sun. You wash your breasts back neck face. With a tenderness I have never imagined, you wash each foot.

* *

Hope makes the smallest world seem bigger.

SUMMER

* * *

Something you taught me to love. Menstruation. Before you, I treated menstrual blood like data I acquired in the field. I put it on a swab, labelled and filed. But blood is blood, and blood is sacred. We use blood to mark the sacredness of our union. You had a dream that you gave me a shirt, so you picked your best shirt and put it on me tenderly, like a mother dressing a child.

"But this is your nicest one," I protest.

"I know," you say, very pleased with how it looks.

I am pleased with it. Then you give me a handful of menstrual rags. Homemade flannel cloth. I like using them, once I got used to it, and I'm washing them in the stream now, hanging rags to dry on a rope made of seaweed.

The line looks like the tail of a kite caught in the trees. A pink stain lingers, flower shaped, on the rags. The shapes of stains capture the imagination: an ink blotch in a Rorschach test, an abstraction where I look for associations.

Today butterflies. Rust coloured monarchs. Wings folded, hanging like a thousand eyes on the leaves of apple trees. By the mouth of the river, the sea washes in. A jellyfish swims translucent and blousie. Kelp washes up in long strands. Thick brown ribbon. Yellow mist hanging in the lofts of the trees. Stillness.

Waiting for the leather-back turtle, one of the world's largest living reptiles. Her favourite food, lion's mane jellyfish, draws her here, her leathery oil-saturated skin makes a blubber layer, keeps her 18 degrees hotter than the sea as she swims into the Pacific north, all 500 kilograms of her wanting jellyfish.

21

Ingrid MacDonald

Sun warms skin. Smell of your sweat mingled with mine. Drying on my arms, the smell is sweet and bitter like vinegar and salt, dabbed on the hairs, pollen powdering the stamen, flowers opened wide, the bumble of a bee. A splash downstream. Large and slow moving. Something on its belly. Come to mama, come to me.

Then she gathers her arms and legs. Rises up.

Standing, a human, a giant woman, waves and walks toward me, saying something.

"What?" I say.

"It's me!" the turtle woman says.

This is strange. A face but it's abstracted, a Rorschach with no images coming from it. "Who's me?" I ask.

"Me. Me. Lina!"

"Lina?" Lina. Curtain of electric words, how are you, bouncing back, falling in my lap. Smell of you on sun warmed skin. Line of menstrual rags drying in sun. Fear an enzyme released to every cell. Screaming in the cells.

Disappointment registers. "Aren't you happy to see me?"

"Oh yes," I say.

A hand holds the last of the menstrual rags, washing, sweet smell wafts. "It's quite a surprise to see you, that's all. God, you look like you swam here."

"I did swim here."

Lina's hair hangs in black clots to her shoulders. Sea slugs on her legs, wiggling like extra fingers. Scratches and welts. Arms smeared with a thick white oil.

She looks like Medusa on her day off, swimming with bruised skin, her hair matted with seaweed and flotsam. Lina opens her arms and comes towards me. "Kiss me," she commands.

The strange sensation of Lina touching my skin. Coldness.

Overwintering

Study Lina's Rorschach face with no pattern in it. My mouth slack. Heat exchanged. Suddenly a coldness.

Lina pulls back, "That isn't much of a kiss."

"Oh." Rubbing Lina's hands as if to warm them up. "You're cold and wet. Let's get you comfortable first."

"So you aren't happy to see me."

Oh, out with it, out with it, out with it.

"Lina, I didn't want to do this over the phone but I've been with another woman now. Here in the field."

"What do you mean, been with?"

"Lovers with."

Two simple words. Smallest keys to the biggest door.

Lina comes wordlessly towards me. Hands push me down into the water. Knees buckle, and Lina's pushing down, collapsing me into the river, cold water a shock like a burn all across my scalp, down my breasts, how long is she going to hold me for, Lina let go, air no air, nose collapses inward, cold water nails deep spikes in feet chest rattles chest convulses eyes blur red as blood vivid intense Rorschach no associations only intense red conquering redness redness let go Lina, Lina let go.

F A L L

* * * *

The light from the fire shines on everything. My hair wet from washing, I'm wrapped in a wool blanket, legs tucked in, my arms around my knees. The wind rustles red and gold leaves. I reach out my hand to touch you, and you say, "Thank you for coming to me," just as the hawk-owl calls *Tu-vita-vit, tu-vita-vit.* I begin to laugh; I laugh almost hysterically, with the flames egging me, and the wind carrying my laughter up and up. Then I rock my knees against my chest and cry quietly. You let me cry for quite a long time, sitting with me, as if tears are only part of the wind, and this is how it should be.

* * * *

This is my body.
It lived through my own volcano.
This is where I want to be.
My body is a new nest in my soul's tree.

* * * *

This time of year, it's not easy to finish before dark. Dusk sets itself on the ground so early, extinguishing the light as I pack up the day gear. Clouds the colour of almond paste and the whole sky bright as a pumpkin with blue eyes. Down here the leaves thickening underfoot and the smell of a good fire at camp. Never mind that I can't see my hands in the forest's dark, I can see the sky.

Overwintering

* * * *

Several hundred feet away, paddling salmon out of the river with her paws, is a grizzly bear. All of the bears on the island will show up soon and we keep our distance. When the run is in full force, the bears feast, gorging themselves on the eggs and brains of the salmon. The downstream grizzly half-peels the silver grey skin with her paws and teeth, leaving the pink meat — a hundred bright pairs of coral shoes — littered in the shallows. Later the cougars and the wolves and the hawks will come and take the rest.

Mouths of fish are razor sharp thrusting upstream, dangerous as thrown swords. I hold a torch and we watch them in the eddies. The salmon have spent their adult life in the ocean and now come back, come back to the stream where they were born. This is the salmon that was born in this river and this is the salmon that will die in this river where it was born. This is the salmon that buries her eggs in a gravel bed of the green stream, and these are the eggs that overwinter, emerging in spring.

✚ ✚ ✚

The Catherine Trilogy

PART I

Catherine, Catherine

Being the last and accurate confession
of Catherine Margarethe Linck
alias Cornelius Caspar Brewer
alias Peter Lagrantinius
alias Anastasius Rosenstengel
convicted of sodomy, desertion, multiple baptisms
and many other serious crimes
in Halberstadt, Prussia,
the year of our Lord 1721

I fester in this prison waiting for God to tell his mercy to me and show me the way to escape this condemnation. The magistrate wants to put me to death for all I have done to undo the womanly nature of me, and I have begged him not to, for I have done nothing that cannot be fully forgiven.

From my birth I have rebelled against my flesh and wanted to live as a man, for a woman is forever spoken to by life and forever forbidden to respond, but the magistrate has no sympathy for me. He has forgotten me here, a wretched creature with eleven steps from the piss pot to the locked door to the palatte bed, and my feet are cold as clay inside boots, and my arms as thin as whipping canes.

I was born to a peasant family in Gehowen in 1694 and we ate heavy bread everyday. The bread was barely enough and I waited for something to happen that might change my circumstance, all the while watching my beloved mother carry stones and grow crops, humiliated by the dryness of the unyielding earth. I saw how my life would emulate hers with its meagre harvest and how sorrow would echo through my face into the faces of my children.

Ingrid MacDonald

I remained chaste, working beside my mother in the fields and sitting near her feet at night. The day my mensus first made a stain between my legs I hid my face in my mother's skirt and poured out all the grief in my heart, for I longed for heaven to swallow me and take away my womanness and spit me back out on the earth, spit me out even as the lowliest man in Prussia, for there is more freedom in a wretched man's life than there is in the entire lives of five strong women.

"I shall find a kind husband for you," my mother said.

Unconsoled, I told her how the fanciest woman I know, Mrs. Krauter the Lutheran wife of the burgher, must lower her eyes and keep them set upon the shoes of her husband's feet.

"Be careful which wish you wish," my mother sighed and said, "It might come true."

That October a big white tent appeared in the first field east of the village and the Prussian flag flew from a tall pole. The news that recruiting officers had come to call men to serve Frederick William our king spread through the whole county, and my father and several other men who worked the fields and wanted to make the harvest ran into the woods and hid.

Frans Erbst who played the organ maimed one of his eyes and Hans Fruling who had just married put an axe through his foot so as to seem unable. Max Kunst our neighbour offered a bribe so large it ruined his whole family of everything they owned, and even then the officers saw fit to take the money out of fingers they had bent back and broken.

Only I wanted to give myself to the military's wooden table inside the white tent and longed to wear the buttons of a Prussian soldier's coat and knew those would belong to me if I had a man's name and a set of men's clothes to enlist in. I begged my mother for something to wear, and she slapped my face, so certain she was that the recruiters would kill me the instant they saw me. But I argued with her that I was tall and could style my hair and lower my voice and convince them to take me. We fought all night in bitter tears. In the morning there was a set of clothes laid out for me, and I binded my breasts and stood tall, and the men at the table in the tent hardly looked up at me. There was no uniform either, and I began my career with a long and irksome march north, frozen and stiff at night by my freedom and following the barking voice of an officer who spared no cruelty when he told us where to stand and where to sleep and not to speak and not to think.

Soon I carried a musket, was given a buttoned jacket and knew my commands, practising and drilling but never seeing any battles, for an army was what the king wanted all of Prussia to become for the sake of his fancy. Sixty battalions of infantry and one hundred cavalry squadrons and sixty thousand garrison troops were recruited from the fields and yet there was not a single battle to fight. My life drained from me like an untilled field and grew sluggish with shouted commands, constant drills, the threat of punishment, the mouldy bread and the wet ground that served often as our bed. I served Frederick William for three years, when a letter came telling me my mother was gravely ill.

Wearing my buttoned jacket I went to my captain's tent and begged to be set free. He looked up from a lighted table full of maps and explained how I could not go free as the king wholly owned me. "Then give me a leave to see my dying mother," I said.

"I know your type," he said. "If I let you go you'll never come back."

"Please sir," I said.

And he said, "Stop asking now or I'll have you disciplined."

Ingrid MacDonald

I was so angry that night. I left my buttoned jacket on the ground and stole away from the troops and took to the forest and ran all the while jabbing my palms with brambles and thistles, and didn't stop running until I could lean down and wash my eyes in the waters of the Rhine.

I walked along the banks and saw a ship at mooring. Not far away, underneath a windmill, sat a red-eyed merchant marine. He was very drunk and welcomed me with a fierce grip of his hand on my arm. I asked for some drink and as I can tell quite a tale if there's something strong under my tongue I passed myself as a sailor to him and told him of my mother and asked if he were southward bound on the river. He grew fond of me and invited me along. At dawn I went to board the *Maria Magdalena*, the mist covering her seven sails. I held my arms open for her to carry me south to my mother. But there, on the wooden dock, was the Eighteenth Infantry Unit of Frederick William's military garrison, waiting for me, full uniforms, muskets cocked.

I was flogged and would have been killed that day had I not begged for confession with a Catholic priest. I wanted mercy for my soul, for the sake of my dying mother's peace. The ancient priest held my hand gravely. "Concern yourself now with your soul, my boy, and forswear the corruption of the flesh." I poured my heart to him and told him my true nature, but he only shook his head. "It is not for a country priest to oppose the will of Frederick William," he said leading me to the noose.

For the sake of my mother, I begged him to tell the regiment command of my nature but he refused, shaking his sad head. When the noose was lowered onto my neck and I began to weep unrestrained tears, I saw the priest whisper to the presiding captain, and then they argued between them for a minute until the captain called halt. The captain took the hangman aside, who

Catherine, Catherine

in turn took his hood off and gripped my face in his giant hands, crushing my cheeks, certain he was being tricked out of his day's work.

In the end I walked away free though fiercely abused and forced in the clothes of a woman by the captain and assigned papers naming me Maria Schmidt. The captain invented this name when I refused to call myself by any name other than Anastasius Rosenstengel, the name I enlisted under. The hateful clothes of Maria Schmidt I wore all the way back to the village where I was born, only to have the neighbours point me towards the city, where my mother had gone to hospital. Then I wore those clothes into Halle.

Halle was a city of twenty thousand people, one gate, a fever epidemic, and a maze of narrow lanes eternally crisscrossing. The laneways wandered and turned like the wedges on a sundial that shift as the day lengthens. I asked at the shrine of the virgin, at the apothecary, at the water well, at the buttermarket, and then again, always moving inward on a spiral, I asked at the miller, at the butcher, at the weavers, coming into a place where I saw fewer and fewer persons in the streets until at last there were no people, only a tiny wooden door that held the sign of the Jesuit hospital.

Drying plant stalks hung between windows in the narrow lane. A thin cat brushed against the back of my legs. The sound of my knocking and the door opening.

"You can't come in!" a monk opened the door slightly and held it shut. He resisted me with all his might and would have kept me out, if his arms hadn't collapsed. His eyes rolled upwards as he fell to the floor. His arms were ragged as hemp, red pocks marked his body, his lips were cracked dry, and his skin was yellow as wax.

35

I called my mother's name and followed a faint reply, past empty beds and up a ladder. My heart welled with sorrow when I saw her, for she was the last being left alive, and even then she was barely a cadaver with a small bit of voice in her. Her long hair had fallen out in clumps making a nest around her. Her teeth were gone, the skin covering her nose had rotted away, and her eyes seemed not to recognize me.

"Do you know who I am?" I asked. The yellow smoke of fire smouldered in one corner.

"I knew you would come one day."

"You need to drink water." I lifted a bucket only to hear hammers striking upon the door. I ran to the shuttered window and saw a physician in his heavy cloak, wearing a full headed mask, the head of a bird with glass beads for eyes, hammering nails into the door, locking it shut. The monk lay at his feet, his face covered by a black cloth.

My mother's soul must have known what the terrible hammering meant, for she fell dead in that moment. With smoke smudging my eyes, I wept. I longed to tell my mother so many things, of my soldier's life and the ways of the king who loved a military more than gold but hated weakness more than death. Now death nailed her ears shut and left me alive inside. I cried out to God, for I had tried to live my life chastely and honour my mother and had met only shame and hardship.

Through the yellow smoke an angel appeared to me and took my hand and showed me a cupboard with the clothes of men who once took beds in this hospital, and I put breeches and a jacket and a hat upon my person. They were poor clothes but amounted to as much of a man's dress as I needed to conceal my nature from the eyes of men. Then I took a sheet and lifted my mother. She was skin and bones, small as an unnurtured bird that has fallen from a nest. I took the leg of a chair and held it in the fire until it grew bright as a flaming pillar, and I set it upon the wooden door and let the fire open the door with its red hands.

It was night by then and I waited at a bridge until a man came with a cart. I asked him to take us to the burying acre. On the acre I lowered my mother gently into a newly dug part of the ground and settled with the driver of the cart. He was a nervous fellow who held a rag up to his nose against the stench, and I gave him a little piece of metal my mother carried in her purse. It wasn't a coin, but it might be worth something. So many citizens had died from the fever, the ground was a fierce sight, churned and steaming, like when the butcher throws a pail of offal into the ditch. I waved goodbye to the cart driver, though I did not know him at all, but there was no one left I wanted to say goodbye to.

I walked in the direction south, away from the city of Halle, leaving behind its encircling streets and hammered shut doors and the swarm of its fever that sets upon the body like wasps into a grey paper nest. At daybreak I ladled water from a trough for my thirst and looked back towards the acre. I imagined how each corpse was a brick and how so many bricks make a wall and how so many walls make a pavillion and how a great pavillion is being built underground, a huge fantastic building where half of the kingdom, and she who was all my family, now live. I was thinking of something else, but I couldn't remember what that was, oh yes, a name. The name, the right new name for myself.

Nightfall had come on by the time I had walked through seven villages in the clothes of a man, and I was ailing with hunger for I had taken but a mouthful of alesop in the midday. I feared the thought of going to houses abegging. It is known how hostile men are to strangers, especially if they suspect you've come from the cities for they have it they will catch sickness from the mere sight of us. Afar in a field I saw the lamps of ramblers and reckoned they'd be kinder than settled folk and went to ask for comfort from them even if it would be only to sleep near them and not be afeared of the night.

Coming near them I found them not ramblers at all but a group of religious inspirants. They parleyed among themselves with great vigour about the intentions of God and the defiant ways of men. Chief among them was a woman with one black tooth, and she gave me first a stew of boiled roots and a rasher of pig and then a learning in the spiritual way.

She told me her name was Eva and asked me mine. "I have no name at all, for what is it to be named by those who never saw thee as thyself," I said. Eva thought there was wisdom in that and declared that I should have a new name, but first she concerned herself with the more urgent task of purifying me and described how she saw in me a multitude of demons that must be banished.

Thus she learned me the utterances of holy words spake directly to God himself without the nuisance of the priest in between. Just as if God sat in the chair near yours was how I learned to speak. Although I could not discern whether this religion or bewitching be, on account of my soul's salvation I followed her ways and most powerfully her blessing appeared to me.

She asked me if I could be holy and freed my ears to hear by blessing them and speaking many things to me. I learnt a prayer spontaneously, and Eva took me away from the others, to the middle of the harvested oat field, and there among the stubble and stem she lifted up her kirtle and peed into a small cup and took the warm yellow drink and blessed me by pouring it into my hair. "Out, out all besetting demons," she called afore me and then gave me the name by which she always called me, Peter of Lagrantinius, for we were near the village of Langrantus.

My tongue was freed for prophecy, and I travelled with these inspirants by day and slept on the blanket beside Eva at night. I pined for her and might have touched her sweetly but she laughed at my every approach saying she was abstinent for the sake of the spirit, and I should be as well. The deeper my religion went the harsher my love for her felt and I often gave myself the bittermost penances, wearing nothing but a coarse blanket and ashes for the sake of her love. I gladly starved my flesh for Eva's distant eyes and secretly took blood from my arm and drank it through a seive made of her hair, in the hope of gaining her heart.

Our work as prophets in the world was not easy. Coming into towns and hamlets we met with hostility; the folk were routinely savage and called us scourge. Yet among the people there were those blessed by the spirit, hungry for our news, and my task was to seek these out. I had a gift for seeing angels perched on the shoulders of several men or women in a crowd, and I would choose which of these would open their hearts to us. These ones with angels I declared publicly how they were named by God, and they provided us with our sausages and cabbage, our beer and bread.

For my deeds in procuring food through prophecy I was greatly favoured by Eva and remained her chief prophet, speaking always after her on the scriptures and of the peril of man's path in the world, and though she would not take me and let me touch her, I was at least her favoured companion, and we lived as brother and sister chastely.

All was well until one Percy came wanting baptism and to join us in our travellings. Percy was a former seaman, a former importer of spices, a former horse groomer, a former most everything of any manly appeal. He was physically strong and handsome with a moustache, and I trusted him not and so took Eva aside and told her how I saw an evil demon looking out of Percy's eyes. Only Eva chided me for speaking against him, for she said he was a gift to her from God, a gift she had waited so long to receive. I did not fully understand her words until I saw the shadows of them under the stars of a field, embracing in a flagrant pose, and I could not believe how Eva could defile her flesh to lay on her back with that man above her. Didn't she see demons covered Percy pestilent as fleas? In the morning I was sullen and criticized her with a comment about her unkempt hair. She laughed and called me jealous and kissed me once on the lips just to tease me. Forever I rued that moment, for Percy's infestation spread to me, and a demon of lust jumped inside me, and my loins burned in shame and desire.

Soon we went to Cologne where I saw angels on the head of one rat-catcher named Heinrich, and this Heinrich had great wealth in the town for his business had prospered during the infestations while all others ailed, and I prophesied that this Heinrich could walk on the Rhine as the Lord had walked on the sea of Galilee. Only Percy took Heinrich aside and spoke ill of me and spoilt the rat-catcher's faith so that when he went to step on the river he sank directly and nearly drowned and had to be hauled up on ropes.

This rat-catcher was a braggart too — at any time he carried six rats tied by their tails to his belt — so to his miracle he had invited the burghers and all the town to come watch. When he floundered the crowd saw me as evil and turned against me and set upon me. I called out to Eva to defend me, but she knew well the depth of our peril, and away she ran with Percy close behind, leaving me alone with a mob encircling. I tried to flee but they set their dogs onto me and took me intending to kill me with bare hands for the rat-catcher's ruined faith and my failed prophesy.

In sport they cut my man's clothes from me, and when they saw my original nature all the louder did they call for my neck to be hung from a tree. One among them saw a ghost like a shadow in me and declared I was pregnant with evil seed and proposed to the others that the demon-child be cut out of me and spilled on the ground, for a demon-child not properly killed is quick to return, to haunt and bring ruin to the lives of his assailants. Away I was taken to a leather-aproned blacksmith who sharpened his axe against a stone.

Hand and foot they threw me into the smith's hut, and as he sharpened they shouted, "Cut the devil from her," in terrible voices out front. The blacksmith never raised his eyes to meet mine, so shamed I think he was of my nakedness. I feared for my life, and the pain of a knife terrified me until I saw an evanescence in the air around the smith's shoulders.

"Take yourself through the small door out to the back," a voice instructed and then with force! "Run child!" Only my feet wouldn't obey, and I tottered. I felt a firm push from behind that thrust me through a small door, through a passageway and away.

Tired and wretched though I was, I did not dare to stop until I had run for some hours and hidden myself in a dark woods. I was so tired I could have slept where I fell on the ground but the murmurings of wild beasts gave me fear — for what is it to escape the blacksmith's knife only to be devoured by an animal's tooth? I devised that I would have to beg for mercy from some person and approached a cottage where I wailed in a low voice and hid myself so that my nakedness could not be seen.

A man came quickly to the door, and in the light of his lamp I saw how his whiskers stuck out of his face the way hairs poke from the crackled rind of a roasting pork back. I marvelled how his doorway suited him as much as a pulpit for he hardly had the door opened before he began to preach. He described only the evil of the poor who know not how to work and call damnation upon themselves with their stink and poverty, for no one in his esteem could be poor or ill without the Lord having assigned misery unto them, and what is misery if not the due penalty for sins? He preached, stoking the hot hell-fires of his mouth until he had expended all the miserable creatures of the world with his perceptions, and then he shut his door again leaving not a scrap for me to put in my belly nor a rag for me to wear on my naked back.

I was in greater misery than when I had first cried out, and tears came quick for I hated my wretchedness. I tried to quell my tears as soft footsteps came near me, and amazed I was to see a woman whose countenance I had never before seen for she was dark brown in her whole figure, with broad features for her face and hair that softly shaped around her head. I hid my naked person in the hedge regarding not the pain of the brambles. She spoke with a tongue as fine as any good lady ever possess, and I took her as the mistress of the property come to expel me, until she described herself, and then I realized she laboured for this preaching man. Sharp words had she for his miserly ways, "What nature of man is this who spouts pious concern and then breaks the Lord's first rule with his very sermon?" She said, "Come near, Poor Tom, whoever thou be."

"I cannot come near for I am naked," I cried and hid myself further from her.

Catherine, Catherine

"Then you shall have clothes," she said and went away to bring breeches and doublet well-used, although finer in their aged state than my father ever had and a bowl of warm groats that she set down where I might take it. "When God asks of you, report that it was Sabina's kindness you received tonight. I shall pray for the relief of your misery as well," she said, and I gladly took what she left for me and slept that night secretly behind her small cottage, at last to sleep in the comfort of the merciful.

From there I took to wandering in lanes and streets and would have made a career of begging had the Polish forces not come that way towards Berlin with their grievances against the French king. I had no grief against His French Majesty, but the purse they offered a man who could fire a musket to join their side suited me.

The first time I joined the forces I wanted only a soldier to be, thinking soldiers were free. But even they have a bitter existence. A soldier is only free to follow commands, and I wanted more from God than the privilege of marching about with a rifle. So I studied manhood itself and let my desire teach me, and the forces are training ground enough, and the manners of men with their lewdness and shit-stained breeches are not difficult to emulate. Our duties were arduous, with great distances to walk, but never so foul as the time we ruined the cathedral at Liege. The commonest of things cause the common man to rise up, and a cathedral is a difficult thing to take away, for it is owned by all, and it is harder to move a single stone from a man's sacred place than it is to cut out his heart.

The streets were full of persons who fought against us, and the women and the religious the worst among them, shouting names at us, pouring water out windows, smacking us with brooms. We soldiers had to hit them, men and women alike, and

43

break the colourful glass of the cathedral and ruin the glass faces of the apostles and show nothing in our eyes.

All the while I was among the Polish army I concealed my person carefully and was reputed to be shy for I held my piss and shit until I could dump it in private, although shyness among men is fecklessness, as far as they were concerned. While I had none of the membrum of men, I did have the hands of a woman and clever hands too, and still I longed for another way to be. So I took some leather and sewed a long sausage of it and filled it with dried peas and to it added the bladder of a sheep that hung from the bottom of the sausage and fastened the piece onto me with a leather strap that went between my buttocks and around my waist. To this I added a sheep horn, born through with a hole that allowed me to piss from a height as my fellows do, and my membrum virile woggled proudly in my breeches as a clapper dangles in a bell.

Near to Brussels we fought a battle that left the ground a sight to sicken the strongest. I came upon a man named Caspar, a young man I had known and loved, who was very proud of a set of playing cards that he carried in his pack. Face down he was, clotted like clay to the soil, his blood turning the earth black around him in a pool. I wanted a decent grave but we were being hurried on and told not to worry about burials, and I argued with my captain and blamed his stupidity for Caspar's death, and when he disciplined me I struck him back across the face and cursed him. He said I was to run the gauntlet, and I saw the other men preparing to beat me with swords, but I did not give them the chance. I was gone into the woods of night, and they could not follow for they would have to break from their battle to find me.

I travelled secretly, hiding in forests and walking the roads at night, discarding the parts of my clothes that described me as a soldier. On the morning of the third day, when I was weak and hungry, I spied a maiden tending her fields. She was alone, and I prayed in my heart she would help me.

She was Catherine, she told me, and lived in a humble cottage with her mother, her father having long since died. I gave my name as Cornelius, thinking it an attractive name, and amused her with tales I had learned from soldiers. Perhaps I deceived her, although without unkind intentions, when I told her my father was a wealthy weaver in Nuremburg. I never intended to ail her when I described myself as one who imports fabric from the New East for it interested her so much, and I could not foresee how it would bring grief. In turn she delighted me, and we went into a cow shed together, and I tickled her with my substitute, and this she greatly fancied.

Presently we went to her mother to have her agree and then to the parish for the askings. All the while her mother looked at me askance. I knew she took Catherine aside and instructed her how she must touch me just so, here and here, and report precisely what she feels. But no amount of touching would come to any advantage, for I have never had much of a woman's chest, and whenever Catherine stroked my pants my membrum would be there in full virility, erect with its bulge underneath, such that Catherine would have had to blush to describe to her mother how the manness of me held constant vigilance.

The mother had little case to refuse us, and soon it was arranged that she should sleep in her own small bed in the corner while Catherine and I took up the bigger bed in the house that now properly belonged to me. The mother never eased her contempt for me. She was scurrilous as a dog whenever she caught smell of me, and soon I saw the reason for it. In the late afternoon she stood with the afternoon light behind her, and I could see them all there, more pestilent than Percy's, a thousand demons covering her, setting her soul against me.

Catherine's mother's demons always looked through windows at me. Though I did my best to treat Catherine as my wife, it was no use. I entered her with my leather member often and frequently, no matter now it tired me in the effort, for I would not have her complain to the other wives that I had no courage in me. But the soldier's life had ruined me. I worked not, and my tales of weaving and importing proved untrue. I took my business to the public house and drank ale all hours. When I had no coins left for paying, I went to the house and took some such thing, linens or clothes or what have yous, as they all were now rightly mine, and sold it to one man or another for the price of a drink.

Catherine turned a shrew and called me abbeylubber and scolded and complained bitterly how she hadn't any eggs for I had sold everything, even the biddies that scratched in the yard. In return I abused her and clapped her ears with my hand and yelled how her mother poisoned her thoughts and set her against me. When I was home with her she would sit in woeful tears until I went off again to the public house.

So it was, until the night when her hateful mother came after me and sought me in the public house and in front of all present and with her rotten teeth shouted of the womanized nature of me, making a tittle of my affairs. I approached the spiteful woman with my sheephorn in place and pissed a full pint of piss onto her while the other men jeered and laughed. "That will learn you for womanizing me," I said, and the carpenter clapped me on the back and gave me his jug. But when I left off my aleing that night I knew how much ruin was upon me, and I shunned my home for ever and took to wandering in the roads to the southeast.

Thus abegging did I feel the full breath of wretchedness for

Catherine, Catherine

I had become a creature without society, hated by men and women, not at ease in nature either, for I found no peace in the form I was born with. Yet, in my mannish state, what had I wrought but grief? If I have ever woven anything, it was a tale of misery, neither man nor woman and neither able to be.

I slept in cow barns and ditches and asked passers by for a bit of caudle to eat. They called me hateful baggage until a vision of a woman came to me as round as a milkmaid and wearing fifteen rags for her skirts. She recognized me where I lay sleeping and spake easily to me, and called me Cornelius.

This was my own Catherine, returned to me, relating the full tale of her mother's havoc, and she, not wishing to be eternally leashed to so wicked a thing as her mother's tongue, did set after me to rightfully be my wife. Together, we carried our hunger and begged with hands outstretched.

After we travelled for many days Catherine woke with a sickness in her that inclined her to vomit, though she had scarce eaten, and greatly weak she became for she spat up the very blood and bile of her. She was so badly that we went to a parish and described ourselves as Lutherans and begged sincerely for a bed to lay her in, and after a day of waiting, for God watches even the smallest sparrow fall, a room was given us in an alms house.

Catherine stayed in that bed for near to a week, and I did sit with her, and never did we argue. I pitched the phlegm from her spitting pan daily and held her hand. We needed money for making our way, and once she had some strength returned I went about asking in the streets, but the smallest coin made me only think of ale, and when a cleric in a brown robe pressed a coin worth two Reichstalers into my palm, I had no strength to resist.

I went to a house where a fleshly woman named Miss Hilde

spread her legs and let me please her for the price of the first Reichstaler. The second Reichstaler bought me a whole jug of red wine. Filled with wine and bringing my member inside Miss Hilde's legs made me happier than anything in the Frederick William's palace ever could, for everything about her person, her hair, her face, her legs, were opened to me, and I was not wretched in any part of my person, but my legs tingled and my arms sang.

I stayed away the whole day, and when I returned drunk as Davey's sow to Catherine, she put the devil upon me with her tongue for her strength had returned enough to ballyrag me for taking up my old drunken ways and being a wretch who cares not whether his wife breathes or dies, and this riled me for I was full of pride.

Being drunk I had to piss and fumbled with my sheephorn and while standing above the chamber pot dribbled onto my shoes. "Other men piss without wetting their shoes. What is it in you that you can't even piss like other men?" she mocked me.

I threatened her with my fist only to fall drunk asleep before my hand was fully raised. Catherine took a candle then and lit it near me and unfastened my clothing, first my doublets and then my breeches, and felt the soft of my skin and discovered the inanimate nature of my membrum. She was greatly amazed and afraid, for she discovered our natures were identical in every way. Then she took a knife and cut my membrum free and concealed it.

In the morning when I woke I saw clearly what was gone from me, and yet I did not want Catherine to suspect any wrong, so I feigned to have lost a coin in the bed and searched in vain. Soon desperation set upon me for I found nothing.

Then Catherine looked at me from where she stood and confronted me with my travesty and told me how she burned my hateful member in the fire. "Can't you smell the stink of evil burning?" she asked me. I knew that I was ruined and begged her to kill me at once for I feared a riled mob would come to make mockery of my flesh. For that is what they did with the old couple at the workhouse in Halle who were said to be witches. First they tied the thumbs of the woman to her big toes and flung her in the river, and once the wife was drowned, they tied the husband to her corpse until he also was drowned, and the chief tormenter among them collected money for showing the town such sport.

Except Catherine spoke easily to me and called not for my blood. She would abide with me if I mended my ways to live in decency, which I then promised, and this promise I have always kept, and not from fear of exposure either, but upon my honour.

Once Catherine had shown mercy to me, I felt a covenant more binding than with any Lord. Even the Lord who sits beside you in his chair cannot compare with the mercifulness of my Catherine. Of my truer nature we made a pact of secrecy for I still wore my mannish garb and her husband proclaimed to be, and in our lives, where fear might have wrought evil, only kindness reigned. We stayed at the alms house and kept intimate company, and one time Catherine asked me what my name was from birth, but it eluded me and would not come in my thoughts. So Catherine, being learned of most of the alphabet, penned a letter to the parish clerk of Halle, where I was born of my mother, and described me in such a way as I was when I was very young and inquired what the Christian name of this child might be.

We exchanged work for food at the parsonage, and Catherine took sewing that needed to be done for gentle ladies. As I had no tasks myself and being learned by nun's servants of such delicate things, I would sit and sew with Catherine. Soon she gained a reputation for excellent needlework done in half the time that any other woman could do it in. Some days Catherine would feel an itch in her, and we had our intimate ways together again, and I would pleasure her with my hands and freely caress her teats and lie athwart her and bring her thrill on.

One day, in the peak of her pleasure, Catherine reached under the bed and returned my membrum to me, for she had never destroyed it as she said, but put it away thinking she hated it, only to be in the swell of her passion and wish for it once again. So I wore my membrum and mounted her and entered her repeatedly until she shouted with the greatest pleasure imagined.

Then she undressed me, and for the first time I willingly let Catherine take my clothes from me. I stood wearing only the membrum I had fashioned so carefully, and I wondered what it is to be a man, to have arms and legs and a membrum, and what it is to be a woman, to have hands that can express so much. Then Catherine moved gently and knelt before me and fondled my teats to rush my blood and kissed my thighs with her soft lips only to set her lips upon my membrum and take it deep in her mouth. Then the fullest passion swept me such that I could barely stand.

Thereafter I kept my membrum, wearing it always and frequently pleasuring Catherine with it. Soon a letter came from the old parish, and we learned that my name was Catherine the same as she, and there we were, two Catherines, only I was Cornelius compelled to be.

On Saint Boniface's feast day we woke to a scuffling in our room and discovered a rat the size of a badger thrashing. When Catherine stood to shove it with a broom the rat leapt at her and bit her foot and caused her to bleed. She let out a terrible scream, and I took a stick and brunted the hateful beast to its death, only to see its gut run yellow and its blood run green, and both of us were chilled with fears of the worst. Soon Catherine took all ampery and lay with a fever on the bed.

I sought out preparations to help her but without money could not procure any, so I arranged for some travelling marketers to convey Catherine to her mother's home, where she would have money to fetch the physician to her.

A day behind I followed on foot, begging all the way for what I could, crying out of my wife's misery and our great misfortune. I collected a smoked ham and a pot of treakle and was glad to have some nourishment to bring to Catherine, but when I came to her mother's door it was barred against me. Her mother was enraged and stood behind the door calling me scourge and proclaiming the womanly nature of me.

Yet I prevailed against her madness and shouted how I had brought food to she who was the rightful wife of me. Beset as she was by so many demons, the mother stank most foul and laughed at my efforts to bang down her door. Her laughter caused me to push all the harder, and soon a crowd gathered to watch our dispute. I banged and shouted, and then all of a sudden she opened her door and said, "Amends, amends, enter. "

I should have known that demons make only a mockery of promises, for as soon as I entered she fell upon me with her carvery knife and gashed my thigh and tore open my breeches and seized my masculine emblem from me. She raised it high for all those gathered to see and rushed into the street with it, shrieking to fetch the bailie.

In her frenzy, she left me unattended and free to run away, but I did not run. For it would be only a rabbit's freedom, as a rabbit runs free until the tooth of the hound pierces her, and I had

Ingrid MacDonald

no want for such freedom. I longed to see my Catherine and found her in the back room feeling greatly relieved from her ailments. I called out, "Catherine, Catherine, it is me, the one who loves you who comes near." And she called me to her, and together we amended our grief and gave our promise to each other. We kissed and vowed that all that was ever intimate between us be forgotten from Catherine's memory, and our joy as much as our grief be lapsed from her thoughts. The true nature of me, we confirmed for her future and safety, was never by my Catherine known.

PART II

True Natures

Halberstadt
October 5, 1721

Dear Gregorius,

Shadows of cloud passing before the sun streak my desk. I study them, engrossed by their quiet changing and gaze long outside, until interrupted by a servant's knock. The scent of lemon oil in the heavy wood of my desk, the crucifix above me on a plain wall, my own hand emerging from a sleeve holding an inked feather, the yew trees through the window are surrendered to the servant's presence, telling me this infuriating woman is there again.

"She's been at the gate all morning, shouting she was robbed of her pots and linens. Shouting she wants the Linck woman hung."

I gave instruction to chase her away by the dogs. "Make sure she won't return! Tell her I will have her arrested and flogged if she ever comes near here again."

It infuriates me. Is this what the law has come to mean Gregory? A tit for tat that gratifies a hateful old woman's

55

Ingrid MacDonald

vengeance against her daughter and another woman who have stolen her pots and pans? I have the case of the Linck woman before me. I read and reread the argument for prosecution. The charge of sodomy is strange, but I keep returning to it. This woman masqueraded her whole life as a man. She mocked the king when she served in the Prussian forces as a musketteer. She performed abominations with a masculine member made by her own hands. She wore this instrument strapped onto her person, even devised a way to urinate from it. She married a woman, the screaming woman's daughter, and had sexual relations with her using the hateful substitute every time. She took pots and linens from the house of her mother-in-law and sold them for money. The preliminary court may have been fascinated to a fault by the evidence of her *membrum virile*, but I do not feel they have made an error in naming this sodomy. If it is not sodomy when two women come together and mock the order of the world, then what is?

Women are strange. They dwell outside the grace of laws and without peace. These two on trial and the mother that screams at my gate, even my own mother who is not in any way like these others, all live without peace. Mother tries to be devout but falls into despondency so quickly and becomes irritable and weak. She argues with me and bemoans her suffering for she has so many ailments. When I answer that we could call the physician in she disregards me, pretending deafness. Her eyes slitted shut, and her tiny fists angrily wrapped around a spoon confound me.

But this is not why I am writing to you, Gregory. Forgive me this aging man's grief over his aged mother.

I have had a terrible argument with three ministers, and this argument has left me deeply disturbed. We were discussing the

penalty for Catherine Linck who I want condemned and be-
headed. But these three men (you know at least one of them well
but I fear writing their names in a letter, lest the military inter-
cept), who are the wisest of men and all confidantes to the king,
consider her blameless. While we were in session I became so
enraged that they would forgive this woman's abomination only
because she is a woman and does not properly fit into the
definition of the law that I banged my fist on the table. I shouted
at them for their stupidity. They sat passively looking at me
through spectacles. Then I became distressed that I might be
loosing perspective and I took myself away from the table to
gather my thoughts.

I fear these ministers, for they might say something to
Frederick William about me, and as you know, it has been so
difficult since his ascent. He wants to see every trifling that issues
from a court. At first I mocked his intentions, thinking no prince
in all of Prussia has ever cared for a day's work. But Frederick
William is insatiable and reads long into the night, remembering
names and details. And he is cruel with those who displease him.
I heard how a magistrate named Wolken, from Magdeburg,
criticized Frederick William for harvesting so many peasants into
the army that the crops were left to rot in the fields, and there
was no grain for Prussian bread. That very night, when Wolken,
who lectures at the university, walked with a young student, a
troop of calvalry confronted him. They shamed him and trampled
them both so fiercely that the student lost his life. And Wolken
has lost his post at the university.

In truth all Frederick William cares for is his military, and it
is well known how Prussia suffers while he collects his tall
soldiers, which he loves more than anything. He sends his
recruiters to Denmark and France to find tall men. There isn't a

circus in all of Europe with a giant left in it, for they have all been bought and now wear the uniforms of the king's guard. As much as I fear the king, I do not want to let this sodomy charge be reduced to petty theft.

I apologized to the three ministers asking them to forgive my outburst, saying my kidney stone torments me and the pain of it alters my temperment. Then I excused myself to walk outside and went to the place of the punishments. You know well how it is out there Gregory, but this was the first time in many years that I looked with any interest, for I am distanced by the duties of court and never witness the end result of our work.

I came first to a man who lay on a rack, hands tied behind his back, while the handles of the mechanism disfigured his skeleton. Two men poured a jug of water into him such that he gulped to swallow and could not cry out, and his belly became as bloated as a corpse found after three days in the well. Another man knelt with a crucifix held in his roped hands. Above him the sword suspended in the arms of a hooded executioner waited while the kneeling man wept his mother's name.

I walked to the forest where trees are stripped of branches and crowned at the top with a wheel. On a wheel, alone and high above the ground, a man sleeplessly gripped the rungs. He seemed familiar to me, but I could not place it at the time. Now I realize how much this one man, in his shape and height and colour and age, resembled myself.

Repelled by horror yet unable to take my eyes from what I saw, on the wheel and all about me, I saw the terrible truth at the heart of man. What a profound experience suffering is! Gregory, man is, because man suffers!

In the distance I saw the flames of a burning, its dark incense billowing up to heaven. Souls are flying up to God in that smoke, flawed and contaminated flesh returned by the process of justice to the spirit. We are God's gatekeepers here, giving back to God what we cannot tolerate on earth, and the greater judgment waits us all, in heaven or hell.

I returned to the court deepened by the sense of suffering and searched for my ministers, but they had gone without leaving a word. So this business of the Linck woman has been left overnight. I could not sleep, and a terrible dream came to me that in my absence they let the woman go. The king pursues me with the hateful mother-in-law close behind, screaming of her stolen pots. Frederick William is the age of a mere boy but mighty on horseback and dressed in his full military uniform. He is furious with me for failing to punish the Linck woman properly. He takes his sword to cut my tongue out. I woke just as he pushed his knife into my opened mouth.

If only these ministers weren't so literal in their reading of the law! Gregory this is the trouble with Prussia today, for the military mind has taken over and left no room for the interpretation. They wish to command the courts like troops in drill and do not know how law must be always read with new eyes.

One smokes his pipe and draws his stained finger tips through his beard and argues that the absense of semen, which cannot have been spilled or ejaculated from the Linck woman's leather member, does not follow reasoning for a charge of sodomy. "By pressing a lifeless leather object into the vulva of another woman, no penis is abused, no semen spilled and no fleshly union perpetrated." He rolls his eyes impatiently. "Sodomy requires a penis."

The pious man of them, a priest who infuriates me by speaking always in a whisper, says he has consulted his superiors. "Although the Holy Scriptures expressly forbid sodomy between men, nowhere do they explicitly discuss such an abomination between women. In Leviticus it is mentioned that women are forbidden to pervert their flesh in union with animals."

I rallied against him. "In the Scriptures it is described how the Sodomites turned away angels who visited their city. The Linck woman's crimes are not comparable to some schoolboys playing itch buttocks in a shed. Her sodomy let her very soul be corrupted by desire. Sodomy carried her into the streets wearing a dead man's clothes, to steal and prophesize and corrupt other women, changing them into puppets of their lust. The imagination of the Sodomites was so evil that God rained fire and brimstone and devoured whole cities because of them. The prescribed penalty in the Scriptures for perversion between women and animals is death. It would not be too unlikely to use the Scriptures in an analogous condemnation."

But he was smug. "What God did not write, God did not intend."

The third of them, who studied in France where they care more about decorating their mouths with clever expressions than with saying anything intelligent, began, "Perhaps you have heard of women in the far eastern plains, who are born with large clitorises. Among these women penetration and fleshly union can be experienced, and here it could be argued that, analogous to the male experience, sodomy is perpetrated. The flesh has been contaminated with sin. But this is hardly comparable to a leather sock filled with sand and tied to a sheep's liver."

I could tell he was mocking me, but I described how the Linck woman had been examined, and no physical deviation was found. The city physician Dr. Borne and a surgeon, Dr. Roper, examined the Linck woman. They brought in a midwife to examine the defendant's genitalia, for they did not want to look upon that part of her, but the midwife found nothing masculine nor hermaphroditic about her. She has breasts and a large womb. Her vulva is fully proportioned and feminine. The midwife described a disfiguration present on the vulva that is the result of abuse during her years vagabonding. But she was born naturally as a woman, they all agree.

The real obstacle with these ministers is that they do not wish the king to know a woman served in his beloved forces. "If the royal monarch were to learn that a woman was recruited and carried a musket for Prussia for three years, he would be enraged."

"Frederick William's guard has been defiled."

"But that is not the essence of the crime!" I argued. "This woman has made a mockery of the designs of nature and the laws of God! Can a correlation not be made," I argued, "between the explicit sodomy of men and that implicit of women? St. Protius of Basilius has expounded on the teachings of Paul, and he would have it that the punishable sin amounts to the same. She has openly confessed to her crimes. I want her burned alive."

"In our country," the priest whispered, "we allow the convicted person to be killed by the sword first, and then burned. To alleviate despair."

"Then kill her with a sword," I said bitterly.

A platter of fruit and cheese was brought in, and we eased our argument for a moment. Then the first minister, holding an apple in his hand, his long yellow stained nails like claws around the fruit, cleared his throat and said, "And for the wife Catherine Muhlhahn you have asked for second-degree torture?"

"She requires a severer process of justice," I defended. "While Catherine Linck has confessed freely and fully, the alleged wife is sullen and suspicious. The truth has yet to be arrived at, in her case."

He clucked his tongue. "The process of justice should not be harsher than the penalty for any crime."

The priest whispered, "She denies any knowledge of the nature of this woman."

The arrogant one added, "Surely she is a simple woman who has been seduced into depravity."

I could not admit to them how Catherine Muhlhahn is an enigma to me. When I was speaking with the midwife I asked if, in her opinion, it would be possible for a woman to marry another and not detect that the sexual member was inanimate.

She gave me a discouraging response. "Sir, I am so amazed at the ignorance of country people that I truly wonder how they manage to reproduce themselves at all, for they hardly know what part of their anatomy the babes come from, that it must be trial and error and a great deal of lust that gets their members in there in the first place."

The priest folded his hands as he must in the confessional, when he sighs and gives absolutions. "Are you aware that the wife has asked for full acquittal on the basis of suffering she has already endured? Both in the squalor of prison during the term of the trial and the severe melancholy caused her by not being able to come to the aid of the defendant during that time."

This argument provokes me! "The woman has claimed melancholy, but when Dr. Borne was sent to perform an examination on her spirits, she was hostile and vulgar with him. She spat upon him. He saw no signs of melancholy."

The third minister held a green pear in the air, waving it as if it were an actor's prop. "The co-defendant pleads she was unaware of her alleged husband's nature. She reports that her husband's member was always warm and full. She also says that once, when she fondled his chest, which was covered by a shirt, she commented on the size of his breasts. He replied that many men have such chests. As an ignorant girl, how would she otherwise know?"

"It is apparent that Catherine Muhlhahn is simple-minded. However, her own mother says she told her frequently that she doubted her husband's nature, and nonetheless the girl perpetuated her marital arrangement and continued to perform sexual acts with this so-called man."

"She argues that she only followed her marital vow to honour her husband. Clearly we can not condemn a woman for honouring her husband."

I banged my fist on the table again. "Why did she never feel the strap that secured the woman's leather member to her body?"

"She says she was never able to feel it! Because it was kept between his legs, and he always wore his clothes!" the third minister shouted.

"Furthermore the alleged husband was given to demonstrative bursts of violence, and as he beat her often, Catherine Muhlhahn lived in fear of her husband's retributions."

The bearded minister lit his pipe. "During the process of trial, has Catherine Muhlhahn been flogged?"

"Yes. Fourteen or fifteen times."

I ordered every one of those floggings myself, so determined I was to get the truth out of this lying young woman. Her will is so difficult to break! I asked the soldier who I sent each time, if there was a confession yet. "She's some kind of demon, Sir."

"How so?" I asked. "Doesn't say a word at the beginning or end, Sir. And when I whipped harder like you told me to, not a sound. It's eerie. Doesn't even flinch." I didn't tell the ministers that.

But they all looked at me. "Fifteen times and no contradiction evoked?"

I was reduced, but determined. "Catherine Muhlhahn has been known to steal an entire season's harvest for her gluttony — her own mother denounced her!"

The ministers shook their heads, and the bearded one smirked at me. They don't recognize how deeply God's law is imbedded in this world and underestimate me. They don't know that I will go to Fredrick William on my own. He will hear me!

For do you not agree, Gregory, that sodomists are not merely those who misuse flesh for perversions? They are those who reject their true natures given by God.

And this Linck woman is so preposterous. So bold! "Why punish me," she says, "when there are so many more like me?" I try to imagine if she is authentic when she says this, and I think of every man or woman I know and scrutinize them in my mind. The men seem like men, and the women like women, and the differences are clearly defined. The worst of it is that she knows no remorse and explains her every sin in terms of herself. "Because you do not learn," I said to her, "I shall use your death as a lesson to others and start with you and continue one by one until I have you all."

The Linck woman's case is as strange and wretched as I have seen. To her I want to award the harshest penalty. Perhaps in the case of the so-called wife, her ignorance can be considered, and some clemency given. But as for Catherine Linck, I will not let her go. I write to you in confidence now, that you might counsel me, for I want to send a letter to Frederick William quickly and supplicate to him and petition his support. In my heart I know this woman is guilty of the worst of sins, but counsel me my friend, has she commited sodomy?

My honour rests with you,
Hans-Josef

* * *

Halle
8 October 1721

Dear Hans-Josef,
I am moved by your argument and write to you in haste. My brother, I feel you are being called by God to do His will in the world, and I counsel you to act quickly. Your ministers are cowards. They care more about their comfort under the king's rule than they care for God's will on earth. Your instincts, Hans-Josef, are astute and correct, and this is truely a case of sodomy, for the defiance and the sinfulness of this woman is flagrant and unforgiveable.

It is not merely a matter of forbidding women to wear a set of clothes, for clothes alone are not reason for sin. We know how some of the female saints were given to wearing men's clothes. Though the truth has been embellished, we can look to the life of St. Marina who's father became a monk and smuggled her into the monastery as a boy, to keep her with him. After his death she stayed at the monastery. She was expiated for five years after a controversy, when she was accused of fathering the child of an innkeeper's daughter. Upon her death, her sex and her innocence were discovered. It also appears to have been true, that a woman entered the monastery at Schönau and lived as a monk undetected until her death. She is quite popular among devout Prussian women who pray to her as St. Hildegung, though of course she is not an authentic saint.

But the wearing of men's clothes for the purpose of devotion and the wearing of clothes for the sake of perversion cannot be compared. Halberstadt must not become the new Sodom with every crazed woman going about as she pleases, bearing arms and preaching, marrying women and flagrantly taking the places of men at tables and in bed.

This woman is a horror, for she even amended the flesh God gave to her with a mockery of a male member. This is what true sodomy is, for what does the Devil himself do, but parody the work of our Lord?

I hear a terrible uttering in the world, Hans-Josef. The din deafens me! Women are building a tower of Babel for their kind, using their flesh and tongues and hair as brick and mortar, taking the devil as their architect, and soon they will want to run the whole world according to their designs.

Prosecute them as hard as you can. Letting one go free allows her to make a doorway in the world where others will follow.

I leave you in God's good care,
Gregorius

PART III

Seven Miracles

Being the full relation
of the life of Catherine Margarethe Muhlhahn,
alleged wife of Catherine Margarethe Linck

Come sit and listen to me now you angels. You know nothing of the sorrows of women but I will give you some satisfaction to drink and tell you how it is I came to be so angry with God.

When I was a child I was the smallest maiden in our whole county. I was constantly mistaken for a hedgehog when I crawled under the strawberry leaves to gather hidden berries. In blackberry season I needed a rope to hoist myself up the trellis, and as I could pick more than I could carry, I taught the dog to hold steady with a basket. I never liked harvesting after dusk for moths are as large as ravens to me, with ancient, sorrowful faces that sweep at small torches giving me sadness and fright.

I lived with my mother in a house next door to Colleen, who lived with her mother and father in a big family. Colleen is younger than me but she grew so big by the age of her menses she needed two stools, one for each of buttock, to milk the morning cows. When it was too hard to walk she wrapped me in her apron and carried me home from the fields. I could have taught the dog this too but her coat is coarse as cat whisker and sharp as scythed hay. Besides I liked when Colleen carried me.

All the lads ran after her when she carried the mop and pail at Frau Durden's, and Colleen had stories only a large maid could tell. Her arms are like rising loaves of bread, and the lads ate as much of her as they wanted and still had plenty for next time. Colleen's mother is from the east near Poland, and she laughs in the evening, and Colleen's father gets mocked because he puts salt on oats for the cows to lick. But where did parents like that get her? She still lives next door, but in the married way now, with a pack of children and a ne'er-do-well for her man.

My father died when I was young, and my mother is from the north where the New Laws made a scarcity that caused a famine for food and also for kindness. The crowned prince forbade the people to eat deer. So the people were driven out and forced to eat what the deer ate, green bark of trees, soup made of pond water and handfuls of red berries when they could be found.

My mother married my father, moved south where fish leap from brooks and there are enough woven blankets for everyone to have their own at night, but she brought with her the spirit of her people. When people from the north have too much food their instinct is to bury it, letting it spoil, before giving extra to a neighbour. People complain about them, that they are stingy and their dialect is harsh sounding. In the south folk are not accustomed to the way women from the north sharpen the knives of their tongues on another's skin.

I have always lived with my mother, and under the vigilant scraping of her voice the part of me that was me grew small, small and hard as a grey flint. And when I reached the age that other girls married, I was more like a sharpening stone than a woman, and no husband could be found for me, as no one wanted a wife the size of a doll and without any flesh.

My mother forbade dancing in front of the hay-harvest fires, where other girls learned how to fondle a man's legs. She taught me never to parade under the maypole with a foolish gleam in my eye for a lad. When Carnival came my mother stayed us both inside, gave me something sweet on bread, and then we mended our stockings. The only congregating we did was in church on Sundays or on the feast days of saints when we'd make a pilgrimage.

One November, on my name day, the feast of St. Catherine of Alexandria, the harvesting finished, we put our best wooden shoes on and walked all the way to town. In one gate, through the whole town and out the other gate. Me looking all the while at the splendid buttercakes, the dripped wax candles, the bolts of cloth, and my mother's hand pulling me tightly forward. Night came. The sky glowed yellow like metal on a sword. We walked outside the village walls, past the monastery fields, to the gallows.

We arrived in time to watch a young man, with a thick beard and a few fingers missing from his left hand, swing. All about us were torches and drunkery, men fallen down in the mud, men singing. My mother's eyes stayed fixed on the gallows. "It's always a man up there," she pointed with her rosary. "Don't you see Catherine? The flesh of men is weak." I thought of St. Catherine impaled on her wheel of spikes, for I had seen her death portrayed on the sepulchre wall, and if men are put to death for sin, I was certain that women were put to death for holiness, because women's holiness is not by others understood.

Men remained strangers to me. The sight of a thief tugged by a rope until his neck breaks and then left hung has a chilling effect on the smallest soul. I never watched a cock fight, or placed a gamble on a dog race, and I'd never seen a deck of playing cards, though I had heard of all these things from Colleen.

And I heard about them from the parish priest who took

young women aside and reminded us how unchristian playing cards are, as they entice men to sin. The Devil's alphabet is of pictures and not words made, as words are the property of God. In the beginning there was the Word, but the Devil was also alive then, a young and a handsome man, and God loved him. Then the serpent came and tempted the Devil to eat the fruit of the tree that would let him see the shadows under all creatures, shadows that only God can see. The Devil felt desire and ate the apple the snake had given him.

When God walked in the garden, he knew something was ill for the Devil gazed in delight at the ground under God's feet. God became angry, for he saw how the Devil had made himself like a god. God summoned the serpent and cut his arms and legs from him, that he would forever crawl on his belly eating dust. God banished the Devil from the garden forever and forbade him to use words to tell what he saw. So it is that the Devil uses pictures in his book. Then God wept because he found himself alone in a beautiful place, and the garden was empty. So God took a clot of earth in his hands, spat some spittle and made man in his own image.

The following spring, after the frost unchained itself from the ground, but before the wood thrushes mated, I was near my twenty-second birthday and pruning the blackberries at the far edge of the eastern field. Colleen was bleeding the bed red awaiting the birth of an infant, and I worked alone. I devised a web of ropes to skivvy myself about, but had to cover all of me in a heavy cloaking, for the rope rubs and burns the skin. I was more concealed than a novitiate at the Carmelites, my only sight through an unpatched hole in my hood, when I was startled by the presence of a young man.

Though I could not imagine what he thought of me in my

hood and gear, I observed him keenly. He was tall, but slight of build, and had such nervous gangly limbs that I could not discern if he be friend or foe. He ceaselessly hastened the air about him, rifling a pocket, churning the wind. He ran his fingers through his hair and now and then let his eyes look directly into my own. He had a soft urgency in him that I suspected, maybe I hoped, was passion. I know now it is only the look of a hunted man. That look of naked terror, as the fleeing soul presses your eyes closed with the garments of romance, is easily mistaken for love.

While I was still entwined in my pulley, he opened his knapsack, unwrapped a cloth package, and for the first time I saw how handsome a thing a set of playing cards can be. He offered to play me a hand. But I knew he was a mongrel with a flourishing manner, his clothes and gear were muddy, and in my mind I heard the voice of my mother rattling in my ear.

"You've stolen those, haven't you?" I said.

"Nay, I won them in a duel and chose to take the man's cards rather than his life."

I thought of my mother. "Nay yourself. I'm not interested."

"But you are." He smiled in a way that brought my cloaking off and soon the grass was pressed down, and he taught me cards so well I soon won a hand. Just as I laid down the Jack of hearts, who should arrive scolding, but my mother. It caused me to shudder that this man should see what age and ill fortune would reduce me to in time. But he was trained in the military way and bowed so contritely that my mother turned of a sudden and asked him his name.

"My name?" he said, admiring the tangle of blackberry vines with a gesture that let me notice his delicate hands, "My name. Is Cornelius. Cornelius Caspar Brewer."

I watched my mother walk away. As soon as she dwindled to

a speck the size of a sparrow on the thistle path that leads home, I threw down the Queen in my hand and pulled Cornelius towards a tree that Colleen had described to me as having large branches and soft grass underneath. He was not so large a man this Cornelius Brewer, yet I feared my feminine parts might be as small and tight as the rest of me. I had my menses so I was wet between my legs, and we found a way for him to slip inside me. So pleased was I with his smooth skin and this wonderful pushing-tugging deep inside me that we kissed until the evening's soup and bread. Then all twittering, I took Cornelius to our house and announced to my mother our intentions to marry. She made the sign of the cross against her breast, but otherwise said not a word.

We three went to the priest to ask for the banns, and my mother wouldn't remove her curious eyes from Cornelius. She stood with her head cranked when he spoke as if she had never before witnessed a man pronouncing words. When the banns were called in the square, one man, Johannes Fleischer, who is a lout and near to a vagabond, scandalized how Cornelius was father to a child and husband to a wife in a village north of ours by thirty miles. A letter had to be gotten from there, and the parish priest testified no Cornelius Brewer had ever there been married or baptized, and a fortnight later, with Colleen and one of her daughters throwing the corn, we married. I have always wondered whether my mother didn't put an oath in Johannes Fleischer's ear for him to say such a thing. It would not be beyond her to pass a pence or a pint to someone like Johannes, if it meant delaying the moment that Cornelius would join us as the man of the house.

For the first time I was happy. Cornelius and I lived in union, and shortly thereafter my first miracle came.

Seven Miracles

My mother had taken sick. She spent many days rasping for breath in a cot near the cooking fire, and perhaps I was more prayerful at that time because I requested her healing, but in the time it took for my mother to become well, God had shown his mercy to me. I grew large.

All my life I felt myself a smudge on my mother's face, a blemish she constantly rubbed at with her thumb, and this is how I had known the world. When Cornelius came to me with his deck of cards, his tales of fabric spinning and his years in the forces, my spindliness could no longer hold me. The concave chest I wore all my youth melted and two breasts, large and raging as untempered horses, emerged. My legs and arms grew long, my belly round, and I grew invincibly hungry.

My mother rose from her bed, amazed at the size of me. She peered at my figure wrapped in a cloth that could cover a bed. "What are you doing?"

A bowl of cooked oats and barley malt nested in my hands. "Eating."

"Did God put you on earth only to eat five times your share?"

"I'm hungry."

"Learn to pray." She tugged my bowl from me, "Only prayer quenches hunger, and only prayer quenches lust." She made a disgusting sound imitating the noises I made at night when I took Cornelius into me, for she moved her bed since she was ill, and we all slept in one room, and I was as hungry for Cornelius as I was for food.

Cornelius came in and looked about the cupboards. He took linen out and put it in his pack and then whistled with pleasure when he found a pair of leather shoes. He put the shoes on his feet. They fit loosely, but he looked pleased.

My mother gasped. "Take those from your feet!"

My father had been dead since before I ever put a thread through a needle. I could not put a face to his name, but I knew my mother revered him as a saint, and these were his Sunday shoes.

Cornelius snorted and took a place at table and thumped the back of a spoon on the wood. My mother threw herself on the floor, pulling at the shoes on Cornelius' feet.

He stamped on her fingers. "Everything in this house belongs to a living man now and not to the ghost of a man!"

I held my breath and prayed for the Virgin to show me how to love them both, for I loved Cornelius but feared my mother. My duty was to serve him, but my fear compelled me, and when they quarrelled, I was certain I would perish. That night I ladled Cornelius the largest bowl of stew while my mother glared and would not herself eat. In contriteness, I did not eat myself but then I was so hungry that I stole oats from the larder, replacing them with stockings filled with stones, hidden at the bottom of the barrels.

In time, when my legs were the size of satchels on the back of a Royal Post horse, the second miracle happened.

Milk flowed from my breasts.

Milk poured out of me, and Cornelius could hardly drink all there was of it, though he sucked me long after dark. In the morning I woke to find the bed soaked through. As my mother began to stir I ran next door to Colleen and let her four babies suck me. I was still full and in pain. Colleen put her milking gloves on and pulled two buckets from nipples as large and sturdy as two thumbs. In return for the milk she cooked a sack of barley. I ate the whole thing out of a washing tub so big it could have once been my bed.

I used the empty sack to tie my breasts up on me and stopped by the chicken house to bring eggs. Where once I moved freely, gazing out the little chicken windows, reaching up to pull out a broody egg, I now crouched with my body filling the whole aisle and only my hands able to freely move. The smelly heat overwhelmed me, the straw bedding dusted the air, and I became dizzy, almost faint. In the tight coop where the biddies clucked, I felt my belly swell under a deep rumble swim. A great joy leapt to my lips for I never imagined life could come through me. The basket of eggs clattering, I ran to Cornelius, and flung myself into his lap.

The third miracle had come. I was pregnant with a little life inside me.

Cornelius' face coloured, and he grew cross. "Then you've been playing the whore again have you?" I denied it truthfully saying that I'd been to the neighbour woman exchanging grain for milk, but Cornelius raged. He cried out to God. He pulled his hairs on his chin, brunted his hands against his own arms and hit his fists against his own legs.

My mother came upon our quarrel and said, "What have you made of yourselves?"

I said, "I am with child."

Cornelius said, "You are NOT! You are NOT!" Then he left the house, staying away until supper the next day. All night I swept the floor with my long hair and wept as an infant weeps for its mother because I loved Cornelius, and I had a little life inside me and feared he would never come back.

Cornelius returned the next night, remorsefully and carrying a gift for me, the only one I ever received from someone other than God.

Where he found it I don't know, but he gave to me a mirror, with a glass clouded and so obscured that I would have better admired myself on the side of a scrubbed kettle. Cornelius held me close and described how the clouding was caused by its properties of magic.

Looking in, especially after a time, I saw my own face reflected in beauty, and the parts where I had to imagine some aspect of my cheek or eye or lips doubly beautiful. I gazed into that blurry realm until I saw not only my face clearly, but Cornelius' as well, and the room around us, then the house, then all the thatched houses in our town and the fields outside the ring of walls all the way out to the gallows. At the gallows I met a young woman weeping. I asked her why she wept.

"Because no one can see or hear me."

And I said, "But I see you."

I've known miracles in my life. Seven miracles are given to each soul in a lifetime, and many people cheat their souls and never even use one, but a miracle is a gift from God and different than magic. Magic does not come from God the father, nor even from Mary the mother who hears the cries of those in despair, but from a person's heart. A heart is a deeply woven thing, woven upon itself as a labyrinth is, and seems tangled and dark until magic lets you see your heart as clearly as a path found in the woods.

My mother came upon me. "Frederick William's own daughter aren't you imagining yourself to be?" I feared she would take my mirror and secured it in the folds of my skirt only to hear that she had another plan for me. She described how she suspected Cornelius a woman to be.

I was amazed.

"Cornelius shuns intimate company and never shows his parts though he must have to piss like any other man. His beard is feeble, his person slight."

Then she questioned me in vulgar terms, about how warm or

wide his member felt when he took himself into me. I thought her mad, and when Cornelius came to table that night I mocked my mother openly.

"My mother is so jealous and perverse that she wants your male member to see."

"I will never wave my blessed cock in your depraved face," he said.

And she answered, "Because you haven't one."

Outside, the sky had a few streaks of yellow and green light left as evening was almost fallen, and Cornelius arranged that my mother should stand across the garden from him, with the hedges blocking the light behind him. He undid his leggings.

"But it's all black!" my mother sneered.

"That's how it is with men," Cornelius told her. "When boys are small their members are pink, but they darken with age."

In the morning my mother still scorned Cornelius, calling him thief for every morsel put in his mouth. I thought only that jealousy had made her lose her perceptions, such that all the world seemed an enemy to her. She interrupted the affairs Cornelius and I began, such that we had to have our sexual relations long into the night and quietly without a gasp.

Just before Easter my mother went to the oat barrel and found a dusting of oats over a barrel of stockings filled with rocks. Cornelius and I were still asleep in the early morning when her rage came towards me, and for once I raged back, for I had come to know my hunger as a part of me that I could no longer diminish. My mother was beyond reason and took my mirror from my things and smashed it over Cornelius' head. Blood poured from his forehead, and I cursed her. Only Cornelius was hardly hurt and proved invincible, and the two of them began hitting and fought bitterly.

My mother called him "Woman! Woman!" and grabbed a knife and aimed to pierce Cornelius between his legs, but Cornelius was stronger and beat her with his hands and put her outside the house and bolted the doors. She screeched so loud she could be heard all the way to the cathedral, damning Cornelius, cursing me. She raged all day, and when it was dark, she finally quieted with exhaustion and then slept in the workshed that night for none of the neighbours wanted her in that state.

If Luther had given me an axe I would have put it through her skull that day, so angry was I with her for always trying to take away. I wish now I'd done it and changed the course of these events, for she took my dreams from me, wanting me to live without the eyes of another in friendship or passion. To live without dreams is to have a stump of wood instead of a tree for a heart, and this is what she wanted for me.

Long into the night, Cornelius paced in the house. Like a trapped wolf he moved restlessly, staring at the shuttered windows, unable to sit in his chair for longer than a moment, muttering to himself. I went to him, his arms leaning on the wooden table, an exhausted soldier on vigil duty. I stood in a doorway, a single candle lit the dark between us.

"Cornelius. Are you a woman?" I asked.

He shrugged. "What choice do I have now?"

In his eyes I saw hunted exhaustion. Those eyes spoke a truth that made the whole world shift underneath us, as if the earth itself were rising on a wave. There was a terrible quiet as the plates of heaven creaked the stars to new positions. My heart knew the truth then. That Cornelius was a woman, and I understood clearly who I was then and what that meant for both of us.

"Come to bed now my man," I put out the candle. In bed I

held him close, though he lay stiff for hours, with his back turned, and when I woke in the morning the bed was empty.

I was in great pain. A clot of blood the size of a goose egg passed from me, and I hated having Cornelius gone. I bled heavily, no longer pregnant. On the path out front I heard that Cornelius had been seen in the ale house, but I knew in my heart he was truly gone.

I longed for Cornelius and suffered my mother who restored herself to the command of the house. I suffered the pain of not knowing what to do. From my corner of the room I saw how small a being she was, little and scrawny, but anger burned in her with the intense heat of a harvest field set alight. From her a charcoal cumulus rose upward. I dreamed of a walled garden where two terrible dragons lived, and I had to kill one, but only one to save my life. If I killed the wrong dragon I would myself die, and both were so fierce I could not know which dragon to kill and which one to let live.

With the vengeance of a murdered queen, my mother governed me. She locked the larder that I might not eat of it and took Cornelius' place beside me in the bed at night. Throughout the days she ordered me with a stick, and hit me if I wavered or tarried. She gave me broth of boiled bones to eat and on Pentecost Sunday, as a solemn procession walked, their decanters of incense swaying, she dragged me before the priests and the nuns with their covered heads and pulled me to my knees by my hair. "This is my daughter. She's so holy she found herself a woman and married her!"

From next door, over a little fence, Colleen saw how I declined. She took me in quietly and gave me food to eat. "You could move away," she said suckling a babe with one arm and stirring a stew with another.

"How could I do that?" I said.

"You could change your name, find a sensible man to marry. Stay away from trouble."

"She would come after me," I said of my mother.

"People find a way," Colleen said, looking long outside. I wondered how much she knew about my life with Cornelius, but I was afraid to say more. We talked of other things, and soon I had to go before I was noticed missing.

Though my mother tried to starve me and likewise I tried to shrink myself out of her sight, and though I worked ceaselessly in the fields and felt hunger so real it became another of my limbs, I did not grow small.

That was the wonder of it. I stayed big when there was no food feeding me, and then the fourth miracle came. The Blessed Virgin Mary mother of God who intercedes for those who have recourse to her, appeared in a dream. She lifted her mantle and out of her sacred vulva produced an egg. On the egg was a compass and the Queen of Heaven carefully showed me how the needle of the compass pointed east.

I woke. Without waiting for dawn, I climbed over my mother's snoring, pinched body and took the road from the village that leads east.

After a fortnight, I found Cornelius, slumped in a ditch outside the west gate of an unfamiliar town. A terrible funk rose from a few open sores on him but our time apart had softened his heart, and he kissed my hand and turned his hat upside down on his head as a clown in a pageant would.

"Madam, come you searching for your king?"

"Aye. But my king is a humbled man."

"Indeed he is. And may his soul prosper from it, for no other part of him has."

I laughed, and it had been raining, and we were both truly wretched.

Begging supported us. We planned to walk to France and begin a new life there. All the begging day we talked of our life there, learning new words for the names of things. But a dampness got into my chest, and I coughed ceaselessly, braying like a donkey. Soon I coughed blood, and we had to ask for a bed, for I needed to rest.

While I slept, Cornelius went out to beg some food, and I felt our troubles were behind us, for I thought they were my mother's doings. Only Cornelius came home to me much too late that night, smelling of womanly perfume under his drunkenness. We quarrelled bitterly. I scolded him as harshly as I could, and when he fell drunk asleep I despaired that there would be no end to this suffering between us.

So I took the knife that hangs from my skirt, carefully undid his leggings and opened his shirt. I took off as many of his clothes as I dared without waking him, and I examined in wonder the instrument she had made — the member which she had carefully sewn and the ingenious piece of horn. I cut it from her and concealed it. I hid these despairing things of hers and returned to Cornelius, to touch her skin with my light fingers and kiss her and press my cheek against her soft chest and rest myself between her breasts in contentment.

In the morning fear visited us both. Cornelius made me so angry because she wanted to squander falsehoods and lie and lie even when it was obvious that I knew her true nature. "What is known is known!" I shouted.

"By everyone?" she said in great trepidation.

"By me! You stupid woman!" I shouted, and then something in Cornelius changed. She knelt and took my hands and said she was sorry to me, for all the pain she had given me, and repented her wretched ways, and asked my forgiveness for treating me as the most wretched of men would. This was the fifth miracle given to me, for thereafter Cornelius changed her ways, as if born from one life to the next in a single moment. She touched me and loved me deeper than God.

Though we were often intimate, and Cornelius showed herself to me as my beloved, she always forbade me to see the feminine parts of herself. In the bed one day, with much softness, I kissed her skin and asked to see that part of her. She did not want me to, but I gently insisted until she agreed, and when I saw it, I understood her deepest sorrow.

She told me softly, "I served under the name Anastasius Rosenstengel and fought for several months in a force, but soon learned I could not bear to always march about in fear of the king. I deserted on a night without moon and followed the glow of a fire across a field only to find a gang of robbers warming their hands. I wanted to have a drink of spirits and feel free but drank of the wrong man's mug. Soon I found myself in a quarrel with a brute twice my size. I fought as well as I could, but I hadn't eaten much in days and was weak. Then he wanted my buttoned jacket as a trophy and claimed it with force only to discover the feminine nature of me.

"There was much cavorting and howling. The largest of them held me down and took fire-hot needles and tattooed my vulva with one of the few words they could spell, WOMAN."

The imagination of cruelty is unrelenting, and I kissed that part of Cornelius to send away the misery those needles had pierced into her, and as I did, a sound came from her that was like the crying of a babe when it is young.

"I was so devastated by their violence that I returned myself to my regiment and confessed to desertion. My penalty was fifty lashes of the whip on a bare back, which I endured all the while holding my shirt to my front, lest anyone see my breasts."

After that Cornelius served two and a half more years, only to desert again. Thereafter she wandered and found her way to the village where my mother had come from the north so many years before, where I have always lived.

Once I felt better from my illness Cornelius liked to please me with her stories and I took in sewing for wages, and Cornelius, who had been a girl in her youth and whose mother loved her, had an excellent hand for reweaving delicate threads in a fabric. We kept Cornelius a man, and the women I did work for were impressed with my speed, and the quality was good, so I charged a *pfennig* or two more. Cornelius would put her hands all around my big belly and her mouth on my teats and her fingers down between my legs where she would bring me towards pleasure until I gushed my waters.

On a day when the sun got dark early, we were having our ways, and I gave Cornelius the leather member back. When I first took it from her I thought it the source of all our troubles. But as God and the angels move through the world without bodies, only the spirit can change the flesh. Her heart was with me, whether she was a woman or a man, whether she had a leather member hanging from her belt or not. I gave her that member back because it was a part of who she had made herself to be in the world, and I felt my love for her, deep inside me.

I never learned what our life would have been like if the wheel of our fortune had not swung and taken me ill again. Without money, we imagined I would be better in the house of my mother where some medicine could be brought. So I went seeking medicine and found only poison when everything was taken from us, at the house that had been our own.

I am older now, and our lives have never left my imagination. I talk our lives to God when I draw the water. Although God has blessed me with seven miracles, I have not forgiven Him for what He let happen to Cornelius.

When my mother returned to the house after trying to fetch the bailie, she arrived with Frau Peterson the Catholic wife of the carpenter, and in the time that the bailie took to come, they separated me and Cornelius. I was locked in one room where I beat my fists to blood on the door, and Cornelius was taken into the other room. These women hit Cornelius' head and kicked her so brutally that, when the bailie came, Colleen's man from next door had to be called to come. He was needed to carry Cornelius, which he did gently.

Then the bailie said, "The wife will have to come too."

"Of course as a witness," my mother offered.

"The evil of the one is the evil of the other in the law's eyes."

My mother unbolted my door, found me on the floor weeping and said, "Here she is. The Devil's whore."

And all I can say is how language is an empty and useless affair if that is the only name there is for me. I was brought to prison but separated from Cornelius, though we were both women by then. Nails were put under my skin and my back beaten until God brought me the sixth miracle. I shrank in size. I became quite small again. That helped. There was less of me to torture, less of me to feel pain.

Now I know how everything real is called by a name. In prison they had names for what Cornelius and I did that I never imagined. I can be with Colleen who is older now too and has some trouble walking. We'll be coming the long way home, and we can say every word we know, including the new ones that have come from France and the north, and I still have nothing to call myself but a woman and a wife and sometimes Catherine. The knife hanging from the belt on my kirtle is called a keeper. The mud that catches under the wooden heel of my shoe is called a clot. The straw roofs on our houses are called thatches. A day's work is called a measure. A nipple is called a teat. A dog, a mongrel. You angels are called by the names God gave to each of you before He made the world in his own likeness. The Devil is called by so many names that we each choose our own to speak of him. When I speak of the Devil, I use my second husband's first name, which is Simon.

Simon is a disciplined and a stupid man, a jailer whose first wife drowned herself in the east pond of the village. Now he is my second husband, this Devil Simon. He has thick arms and considers himself my first husband, and that is as much as we have discussed of what happened between Cornelius and me. I cook and work four fields for my second husband, and in return he pierces my backside until I bleed.

He and I met when Cornelius was taken up the hill. It is the court's custom to have other prisoners brought to watch their fellows perish. They call these things outings, as if they are pleasant rovings in the woods, but they are meant to put fear in the sinful, who witness an ordeal so soon to be their own. For my outing I was placed in chains and fixed in a cart drawn by an ox and driven by him, this jailer I did not yet know but later married. Everyone from our village, including my mother, was there. Colleen came running to me and held a mug up to my lips and there were tears in her eyes, "Poor baby, look at you! Drink this," and sweet wine was in the cup.

Others that knew me averted their eyes and tugged on their

children's ears to keep them from me. Those who knew me not called me filth, and a group of boys scooped the steaming clots of the ox and smeared it on my fettered arms and face. My jailer giddy-upped the ox and said, "At least this will learn you right."

Before I saw Cornelius brought to the block I wanted the last miracle to be for her, that it would be over quickly, and she should not feel pain, that she would not know despair. The driver stopped the cart some distance down the hill, and I was glad to be faraway, where I could avert my eyes. But one glimpse of Cornelius, with ropes binding her arms and bruises disfiguring her face, brought fire to my mouth and a shout shouting, "No! No! NO!" I didn't care that all the plain and miserable heads of the village turned towards me. I screamed, "Woman you are my love!"

Hearing me, Cornelius woke as if from a morning's sleep. She resisted the grip of her handlers and struggled. She cursed the souls of her executors and called on her God, and the axe had to be brought down many times before her head was severed, and blood spattered everywhere, and her screaming was more terrible than the most frightening dream.

I had already become small, but in my fetters the vision of Cornelius so mistreated melted my hands until they were tiny hands, tiny as the claws of a small bird. My vision fell away and darkened, sound receded to a muffled drum in my ears, and when I woke I was on the floor of my cell. Soon the magistrate came to me with his ring of keys and heralded the seventh miracle.

The court had decided I could go free.

"The process of justice should not be harsher than the punishment for a particular crime," he said. And I had been in that forgotten cellar for longer than a year, with Cornelius separated from me, my body whipped every fortnight to coax some confession out of my mouth, and in that time not once did I understand the methods of justice.

"The court also strongly endorses the proposal of marriage from Simon the widowed jailer," and I said, "What proposal is that?"

"The one I am telling you of now."

"Is this a condition of my release?" I asked.

"Not exactly," he said, looking around the cellar, a handkerchief raised to his nose, "but it is strongly recommended. To prevent future problems."

I looked at that cellar. I could taste my own vomit before I could imagine another breath inhaled in there. I took the offer, not knowing I had even seen this man.

"Go and sin no more my daughter," he said. I wish my last miracle had been a cold blue sword from a rebel angel so I could have chopped his soap-smelling hands from his arms.

When Cornelius was taken up, with her went all her words for things, and I never bothered to gaze in a mirror any more either, though we have better mirrors now that show every eyelash in detail, only I get no pleasure in seeing in my face what I have become. When I feel my emptiness down there, where Cornelius' hands used to be, her silken tongue, I swear by Mary the mother of God I don't know what prevents me from lighting the broom and setting fire to every thatch in this village, beginning with the thatches over my second husband's head and ending with my mother's house.

I do not know what prevents me.

Colleen perhaps. How the prophet begged God: if there is one holy among them, would God spare the whole village? I could spare the one holy among them, spare Colleen and her brood of children and her man who carried Cornelius, pass over all of them, as the angels did in Egypt, for Colleen's mantel is painted with the mark I recognize, the blood of women whose holiness is not understood. Yes. Come with me now, you angels. I will divert my heart no longer. Yes. Here is my broom, and here is the fire.

❀ ❀ ❀

Aardvark to Annalida

It's true they'd been fighting. About the ironing and the abortion caravan; about Mary Magdalene in *Jesus Christ Superstar* and *Chatelaine* magazine; about Pierre Trudeau and my open-concept classroom; about Colville's *Horse and Train* and edible oil products and Zeke my dad being a square and Abigail my mom being for marijuana and about me and whether I should know about sex or not.

I didn't know about sex. I knew some words, handy around kids younger than me, but useless near any adult. As for their fighting, I didn't know that fighting meant anything. I admired Zeke and Abigail for trying to find a fair way to share the ironing and thought they were only raising their voices for emphasis.

Me and Zeke and Abigail didn't agree on much. Only one thing. The slogan of a poster on our kitchen wall. It was a family motto for us, like a coat of arms. Zeke and Abigail bought it at the drug store: a picture of the shining sea, a beautiful sunrise and "Today is the first day of the rest of your life." I taped it beside the clock that Zeke kept forgetting to fix. It was twenty minutes slow. Underneath them both, was a basket of clean laundry waiting to be ironed.

The basket had been there ever since Abigail came home from

seeing the rock-opera *Hair*. She went by herself and didn't tell
Zeke where she was until she came home. They had a fight about
that. Then she bought the record album, memorized all the words
and started to let her hair grow out.

All that June I watched her beehive deflate and sink under a
spiral of loose fronds. Her natural hair uncoiled around her.
When I asked her to brush mine for me she burst into "especially
people who care about strangers, who care about evil and social
injustice," but she never did get to my hair.

In time I found a way of washing my hair that required no
combing. I borrowed her Herbal Essence shampoo and washed
my hair in the same braids I always wore. Wet clumps hung on
my shoulders for hours afterwards but it saved me the struggle
of combing through nests natting in the back. Soon the parts of
my hair not in braids became frizzy and flew up like pompoms.
It couldn't have looked all that bad because one day Abigail
looked up from the couch where she was reading a feminist
cookbook called *The Edible Woman* and said, "Your hair looks
nice like that."

Our family troubles all began when I asked Abigail to make
Chicken Cream on a hot day. Hot as a July firecracker on the last
Saturday in May, a day full of cicadas zinging from the weeping
willows. Abigail said I could pick the dish as it was a special day,
and she would tell me, later, why.

Abigail's Chicken Cream is a cross between a Waldorf and
an ordinary chicken salad. The recipe was in *Canadian Weekend*,
the magazine that comes with the newspaper. Abigail was in the
backyard, hanging laundry on the line, and the magazine sat on
her clothes-peg basket.

She pointed to a picture of two men, nice looking men, one sitting in a armchair, the other sitting on the arm of the armchair, leaning close to him, by his side.

The wind dragged low, and the sheets slung like railway cars down the length of the yard.

"Get a load of that," my mom Abigail said. "Those two men are married."

I looked and saw a warm red room, with a window and a wall of books. The man in the chair had his hand stretched out, gently touching the sleeve of the man beside him. At their feet a black-and-white cat slept in a curl.

Abigail plunked a clothes-peg into her mouth. "They are married, like me and Zeke. Do you get it?"

I said yes because I believed her, but I wasn't sure what I was supposed to get about it.

Then she flipped a page and said, "This looks good. And it has ketchup in it so your dad'll eat it."

So that was how the recipe for Abigail's Chicken Cream came to our house. With cubed chicken, celery, onion, breadcrumbs, apples, raisins, ketchup, mustard and sometimes Miracle Whip in it. When Abigail said it was a special day, I asked for it straight off without imagining, for even a minute, Zeke my dad would put it in the back window of the car.

Abigail screamed. We were in the white sand parking lot of Sand Banks Provincial Park. Behind us white dunes and green strands like spindly onions waved on the edge of a grey Lake Ontario.

"Zeke, what do you mean? You forgot to put it in the cooler? It's CHICKEN."

Abigail's beehive shuddered on top of her head. The air around her mouth vibrated for a second before the wasps started flying out of her mouth, each wasp lugging a word and each word stinging, and the word "salmonella" so fierce and heavy it needed four wasps to carry it off.

Zeke did his best and swatted what he could.

Meanwhile, the rest of Abigail's body carried on her tasks. She tucked in the edges of the tablecloth, arranged the paper plates. She set out a bag of sliced bread, cookies, carrot sticks, sweet and sours and the margarine as neatly as the breeze would allow. In the middle, she plunked down, in its tub, Abigail's warmed-over Chicken Cream.

None of us could eat.

Abigail folded her arms twice and said, "Well you better tell her."

Zeke frowned and said, "You tell her, it's your decision," and she said, "That's what you always say."

So Abigail said, "Meredith, it will come as no surprise that Mummy and Daddy need some time apart, so we've decided that you'll go with Daddy this summer when he goes on the road. It'll be great. Motels, swimming pools, eat in restaurants all the time. Sounds like fun, now doesn't it?"

For a moment, we held a tableau, a modern *pietà* made of three. A mother, a father, a great distance from me. The distance welled up and became a wind. The sky filled with string, tossing wrappers, pelting sand, and then the gulls came, hundreds of them, tacking in the air overhead.

The gulls swept down and set at our picnic with their claws and their beaks. Devouring everything. After a time, the wind sagged, and the gulls scrammed.

Everything was ruined.

Except Abigail's Chicken Cream, which the gulls left untouched. The wind had peppered it with sand. Abigail poked a coarse finger at the layer of dirt, "Now it's ruined for sure."

Zeke looked at me, "You mean you didn't know? Your mom and I fight all the time. We fight in our sleep." He swung his arms back and forth between Abigail and me. He tilted his head back and drained the beer from his tumbler. "I thought you'd be relieved."

On the last day of school, which was also the first day of the rest of my life, I came home and found Abigail on the porch. Heavy mascara emphasized her closed eyelids, and she sat with her legs crossed, chanting, loudly, "I am a child of the universe."

The time was ten after three on the watch of my outstretched hand holding my report card for her to see. A's in all subjects and A-pluses in two, a blue ribbon in the four-hundred-meter race and a special mention for neat handwriting.

I heard my father slamming cupboards in the house. "Damn your women's liberation conspiracy Abby! Where is the damn iron?" It's no easy thing to be the child of a child of the universe and the child of a father who can't find the iron, simultaneously. I put my report card and my ribbon in my knapsack and went inside. "The iron's on the kitchen table," I said. "Where it's been for the past three weeks."

He still couldn't find it. He yelled, "Abigail! Abigail!" His voice sounded as small as a boy's. In each hand he clenched a wrinkled white shirt.

I set the cat down from the table and plugged in the iron.

"What's the matter with her?" he asked the screen-door as I tugged the shirts gently from his hands.

"She's meditating I guess," I said. "Here, give those to me."

97

Ingrid MacDonald

One thing my father would like you to know about himself and his work: he's not just some salesman like the rest.

We've been on the road for two weeks, and I'm quite familiar with his ideas. He tells me them everyday, over the vanilla milkshakes and hamburgers we have for breakfast. "You think I'm in this for the money?" he says making a sound like a breathy inheld laugh in his throat. He's wearing a clean white shirt, ironed by me on a folded towel on a motel night-table. The new heat of the morning sits on the windshield like a spilled bucket of wheat, and the smallest bead of sweat glints like a rhinestone on my father's sideburns.

If I squint and look sideways, he seems handsome.

Zeke smacks his palms on the steering wheel. "I'm doing something way more important than making money, Meredie. If anyone asks you what your father does, you look them right in the eye and tell them, my father is planting the seeds of a revolution."

So that's what this is all about.

The hook of ironed shirts in the back seat, the car-trunk full of encyclopedias, a hundred copies of volume one, the volume you get on the spot when you fill out a form and promise to buy the rest, are part of, I'm not sure which one, but a revolution. A great revolution.

It starts with the first book, and as you send the money for Anthropology to Zoroaster, the rest of the revolution makes its way in the mail.

Out the window of our popsicle-green Skylark, the cows look like great stones fixed at the centre of a field. Cars on the road spin around them like pinwheels.

"What I put in their hands, Meredie, isn't just a book. I'm giving these women an opportunity. A way out of their prefab kitchens, their crabgrass lawns. Their kids won't need that bus ride to school anymore to listen to some crumb-assed-reject teacher who tells them to sit up straight. What I'm giving them is the real stuff. Right from the source."

My father is a good salesman because he follows rule number one: when you're selling grass seed, never sell grass seed, always sell a lawn.

I spend a lot of time by myself while my father works the revolution. I carefully push his shirts to one side in the backseat of the car and settle in to read Aardvark to Annalida. There's enough words in just one book of an encyclopia to last a long time, and if I thought about each entry carefully, I wouldn't read any other book in my life.

The first word comes from another language. From this word, all the other things that can be known in the universe flow and follow. *Aard* (earth) *Vark* (pig). A noun. A bulky piglike mammal with long ears. To my mind this is a very good way to begin a grass-roots revolution. With a sturdy long eared animal that sucks ants out of the ground. The last word is Annalida, which would be a really pretty name for a girl if you never found out it means segmented worms.

"Where the hell are we? Nowheresville. Downtown nowheresville," Zeke said pulling into the empty parking lot of a Big Sky Motel. The "K" had faded in the sign, and Zeke said, "Big Sigh Motel, oh great. Make my day."

I liked the way the motel looked though. Every inch of it, the doors, the windows, the walls were painted solid sky blue. It was a day without clouds at the Big Sigh.

But it was too hot a day for Zeke.

Ingrid MacDonald

Sweat circles already showed up under his arms, and the hotter it is, the harder it gets for him to sell a book. On a sunny day, the problems of September seem so far away, and no one really cares about the revolution.

I watched Zeke go into the coffee shop and lug his briefcase onto the counter. He gave his story about the revolution to the cashier. My father is a good salesman because he knows that every person he meets is an important person. "Let me tell you something Meredie," he says. "There are no strangers in the world, only customers we haven't met yet."

The cashier wore a sleeveless dress. While Zeke told her about encyclopedias, she looked at her nails and drank pop through a straw. Her hot-pink dress looked stretched to its maximum on her.

Zeke returned a few minutes later chewing a mouthful of toast. He carried a chocolate milk and a jumbo cup of coffee.

"See her?" he pointed back at the cashier, now adjusting an eyelash in a flower-power compact mirror, "Some people don't even want to try to improve themselves."

While I rearranged the shirts in the backseat of the car, Zeke set off in the direction of a new subdivision, where piles of gravel and large round storm sewers marked the edge of the road. He leaned forward as he walked, his encyclop'ic suitcase at his side.

Sometimes I wish we had the rest of the set, the whole set from Aardvark to Zoroaster to display on the back ledge of the car. Whenever we needed to know something, we could just reach. Right then I wanted to know what the word *encyclopedia* really means. I figured it had to do with my father and his feet. *Encyclo*, meaning to go around in a circle all day, and *pedia*, meaning to have sore feet when he comes home.

I used some string, spread Zeke's shirts out around me and

made a bright white tent. Then I spread out some towels on the seat so my legs wouldn't stick to the vinyl upolstery, which softened in the sun like red licorice forgotten in a pocket. Then I found the last stick of Juicy Fruit in the glove compartment, broke it in half to save some for later and settled in to read a stack of *Archie and Veronica* comics.

In the middle of the morning, right around the time I wished I had a mini TV in the backseat so I could watch *Dialing for Dollars*, I poked under the seat where we keep my father's trousers neatly folded and checked pockets until I found a dime.

The floors and the walls of the lobby of the Big Sigh were tiled in tiny squares like all the leftover chits of unwanted poker games, but all in sky blue, and the pay phone was located inside the ladies washroom, which was tiled entirely in pink, the colour of melted strawberry ice cream.

"Hi Meredie," my mother Abigail said as if I were only phoning from the corner store, because I had forgotten what she sent me to buy.

"Do you have a cold Mom?" I asked. She sounded thick in the throat.

"Just gettin' up sweetie. Had a late night I guess." She laughed. It was a laugh like Mrs. Corcoran the hairdresser had back when Abigail used to go for the beehive treatment, and I went with her.

Mrs. Corcoran was under the dryer herself tied inside a pink imitiation-burlap sack. She had a sweet-tooth she didn't mind sharing, and she said, "Fetch my purse here Meredie, and I'll give you a lollipop." Then she got me to go to the ice machine and put an ice cube in her mouth because she couldn't do it herself or she'd wreck her nails. Pushing out with her tongue and holding the ice cube between her teeth, she told Abigail about something Mr. Corcoran had done to her and how he says she's ugly and doesn't like the way she keeps house. Mrs. Corcoran swallowed a bit of ice, looked down at her short hands, her bitten-off nails painted orange and drying on a display table, and she laughed.

"Sales are going good," I said.

"Yeah, right. He tell you to say that?" my mom said.

"No," I said not knowing how to ask this. "Mom when we get home are you and Zeke gonna be back together again like married people?"

Like married people. The picture Abigail showed me in the magazine, two men sitting together in one chair. They were married just like Abigail and Zeke, but Zeke and Abigail never sit near each other like that, quietly, looking out at the world, touching on the arm, keeping each other safe, as if they were one thing, as if they were in love.

"You always were one with the questions. To tell you the truth, Meredie, no. No, Zeke and me won't be together, as far as I am concerned."

"But that's not what you said."

"Let's not get into it on the phone, Sweetie. I gotta go. Bill's here."

"Who's Bill?"

"He's a friend. He's helping me."

I never did find out what Bill was helping Abigail do. I went out into the intense yellow of unfiltered sun, back to the car, and opened the trunk. There lay a whole cache of Aardvark to Annalida, plastic fake-leather covers glimmering, gold paint shining on the edges. I thought I would just do one book but a wind as strong as a tidal wave came up behind me, and soon all the books jiggled and felt light in my hands as I ripped the pages out and tossed them above me. The air took the gold and white pages buoyant as wings with brilliant light behind them, thick as feathers, and the gulls came, hundreds of them, plucking at the pages with beaks and claws, *caw-cawing, caw-cawing*.

Zeke returned just then, his hair flat with sweat. A few pages drifted to the ground, where the mustard coloured dust clouded them. He looked in rage at the fabulous sky.

"You said you and Mom needed time apart, and now you aren't getting back together!" I shouted.

"What's that got to do with it!"

"You lied to me!"

"I should be so lucky!" he said. "Abigail isn't running around on you, is she? She isn't throwing you away! No! Meredith, you're young! You can wake up and say, 'Today is the first day of the rest of your life,' and believe it! What about me? Letting her leave me! Letting people slam doors in my face all day!"

He smashed his fists down on the hood of the car, sweat glistening in the little hairs of his neck, slapping one palm against the hot windshield, hiding his face with the other.

The cashier in the sleeveless dress came out from the coffee shop. "I'm gonna lock up for a while. If youse want anything, better get it now."

"No," I said.

She looked at Zeke but spoke to me. "Ice cream bar, cold pop, nothing?"

"Just leave us alone okay?" I said.

She shook her head and flicked the latch on the screen-door. "Had a bad day selling them books, eh? I coulda told him."

The sun burned down on us, and the gravel was so dry it squeaked under my ten-year-old feet. I quieted Zeke as best I

Ingrid MacDonald

could, putting my small palms on his back. His cotton shirt felt like flour powdered on damp skin, crinkled and fallen. I pressed my cheek against his hip and, in the oldest voice I could manage, I said, "I know Zeke, I know."

➤ ➤ ➤

Travelling West

Travelling north: To go west, first travel north. Celia's hand holds its optimistic thumb to the sunburnt highway, and something paces inside me, a dog hungry for love. Leaning on my canvas knapsack, I doodle a song on the neck of my guitar. Summer is an X-ray of heat on the road, translucent, overexposed. In the distance the trucks ripple, their eighteen wheels evaporating into the dotted line. We step up to their cheap cabins, the cheap seats, country music and Export "A"s, CB jargon, radio crackle. When men are that lonely there isn't much to talk about, *over, good buddy*, and they pick us up and let us down and the distance north gets smaller.

Finding Hugh: When Celia laughs she is young, and when she tells me how things are with her, she is old. I am photographing Celia both ways with my eyes when a truck with Texan plates grinds its gears down and opens its doors. A little man sits in its high seats, like a little king, and he waves us in. He brings us through the miles of rust spruce in his truck, and we've never had it so good. Den of red leather, antlers, playboys, cowboy boots, carpeting, a stereo, he says, *Take off your shoes if you're*

107

Ingrid MacDonald

gonna put your feet on the dash, this is my home. The hours drive by, and his hands steer the wheel lightly, *You ever want to learn to drive a truck, you come with me, I'll teach you.* It is a good opportunity, fairly offered, which I decline. I wonder if I've made the right choice though, when I hear how enthusiastic Celia is. *Next year,* she promises with the resolve of a retiring boxer, *next year.*

Watermelon seeds: Another truck is stopped, engine hood up, doors open on the back, a load of fruit from Florida getting ripe, coming north. Celia and I go off and find a ditch to pee in while Hugh looks at the stopped engine. A young man swats mosquitoes, and a woman climbs down from his truck, lifts down a baby and then another child and another. They talk until Hugh shakes his head. He lays down and looks under the body, rolls back out and says something about the brakes being bad but the young man shrugs. It's a company truck. Hugh comes back, *He's got his whole family in there and a lousy set of brakes.* The gravel under our feet is a beach of white stones, bright and dry in the sun. Hugh has brought huge slabs of watermelon for us. He's sad. We spit our seeds on the ground.

Lone Goose: *Don't ever do that again,* Hugh scolds me. He was on the phone when the waitress came, so I paid for the coffees. He walks quick and manlike to the truck and pulls out my guitar, and I think he's turfing me right here at the where the-hell-are-we Lone Goose cafe, but he says, *Can you play this thing or what?* Celia hugs me and rustles my hair, *Of course she can.* The trees are my velvet curtains, and the parking lot my darkened stage.

108

Travelling West

I'm singing as the dusk falls, comforting a man whose pride I hurt when I laid down a dollar for three coffees, and all the songs I've written of broken homes and lonely fathers come to mind. Hugh leans against the cooling chrome grill. I can see in his eyes, how he is proud of me. He says, *One day I'm gonna tell people that you rode in my truck, and they won't believe me.*

Hold it: When you are with strangers, even nice ones, you never know what's gonna happen next. So I'm almost not surprised when, at the Terry Fox memorial statue of all places, Hugh reaches under his seat and pulls out a gun. A gun is heavier than you think, and he brings it out to make a point. *Girls like you disappear in the bush every day on the West Coast,* he says. *Don't go west.* And Celia, forever delighted by the new, says, *Can I see it?* He takes the bullets out, and Celia holds it in her cupped hands for the longest time. Then Celia passes it to me, commenting on its cool hardness, wanting me to feel it, insisting I touch it. It is heavy as a magnet, and I hand it quickly back. That night Hugh pays for the polkadot motelroom and the kingsize bed that Celia and I sleep in, while he curls up in the bunker of his truck. But the yellowjacket Celia took with her beer ruined it, and she cries; she gets sick in the washroom; she begs for a scrap of the love that was hers in the first place. I hold a damp towel to her forehead and wonder if this is what I want.

Breakfast special: The next morning everything is replaced, the sun on eggs, the waitress in the coffee shop setting the tables, filling the sugar. The contractor arrives, to arrange for the load that Hugh has been hauling, a load of fibreglass it turns out.

Ingrid MacDonald

Seeing us, a pair of girls like salt and pepper shakers at the table the contractor says, *Hugh, you've brought your family*. He says the word "family" with gusto. It is a good and wholesome word to say loudly on the morning-after in the coffeeshop. *Hell no*, Hugh says, *these are my girlfriends*. We wave in giggly unison, but this is the last he'll see of us. We are leaving Hugh that day, going further north while he runs an empty truck back south, to bring more fibreglass, to bring more fruit, north.

True north: Celia and I travel north and it all comes true. North through longsleeved days in air opaqued by blackflies. At night the curtain of insects lifts. The air is intensely clear like the glassy surface of a lake, a thousand feet up the harbour of stars. At the gas pumps moths cloud the light around a single lamp, a shifting luminous flower glowing in the dark atop a stem. Celia holds out her thumb to the road, and I follow, gaining whatever courage I never had by being with her. She laughs and says, *I feel like I'm out here looking for love*, and I agree, but it isn't the same for me. What I'm searching for isn't far away, only too difficult to ask for. We travel north until the axis shifts under our feet, and north spits us out, and geography fools us. Suddenly we are south and east again, newborn, foundlings, at the edge of the prairie. We exchange the pursuit of north, unattainable, infinite northness for the pursuit of west. West has an edge, a geographic limit. West is where the sun goes down, west can be achieved, west ends.

The paintbox: The fields are purple, flax, yellow, sunflower, wheat, green, red, poppy, a land of deep colours cut in squares,

110

like the cakes of colour in the child's paint box that I travel with. The sky is so azure it's festive, done up in a parade of clouds. It looks like a prairie main street on a holiday, empty but decorated. Sometimes I take out a piece of paper intending to write something down when I draw something instead. Only a detail, never a landscape, only something small, the way a flower along the road looks maybe, which I paint with the colours in the paint box. It's never a whole picture, and never a picture of Celia, though I want to draw her. I feel it's wrong, that drawing her is doing what a man should do. Once I broke through though, and drew her hands.

Highway Jesus: This is the summer that Jesus carries his giant crucifix across Canada wearing his trademark beard and swaddling clothes. We see him several times on the edge of Trans-Canada, cars pulled over, people talking to him. In the next town we stay at a hostel where I sing for the German girls wanting to comfort them, because they seem so lonely. Something in my voice only makes it worse, and they wring their hands and cry. I look for Celia and find her smoking cigarettes with the woman who changes the sheets. Celia is comfortable with strangers, and the woman has seen Jesus. He stayed at the hostel too, and when he did she saw the crucifix up close and touched it. It is real wood with wheels on its end, to make it easier to carry.

Yellowjackets: Celia's black and yellow pills with the venom of wasps, my red wine, the stink of smoked grass, the highway an addiction of long and short shadows. The mountains come towards us, and our eyes are cheap cameras against them until looking is seeing a rack of postcards at the check-out counter, and maybe I had hoped for something better. But I don't know what. I thought we would be closer out here, away from our families, away from friends, but there's something stuck between us. The hungry dog in me paces, and I have less and less to say to Celia.

The dog: The day I leave her, Celia is standing at the crest of an intense green hill. Near her, the French-speaking boys talk among themselves. They are the soft spoken, elusive and untranslated boys she sleeps with at night. I climb up to her to say *I am leaving in the morning*, but it is a backward way of saying come back to me, and she hears it only in its forward version. The green hill is soft moss under my feet, but it isn't easy to walk away. From the top of the hill Celia holds out her hands, as if they are dripping, as if I could go and lift her up to me. She has lost a contact lens, and I hear her calling me back. Celia shouts, *But I can't see, but I can't see!* Her voice fades as I turn a corner, where a stray dog crosses me and snaps at my hand. I pull away in time, raise my hand; he yawns on his haunches and looks me in the eye.

Travelling west: After that Celia and I travel west, individually.

The valley: By the time I reach the Okanagan valley, it is pouring rain. The arid hills of apple and apricot trees run ochre, mud in gulleys, puddles on dirt roads where the rain pounds its fists down. It is almost sunny through the glassy yellow rain. I stand outside the rain, in the doorway of a small church. Across from me a hamburger stand sells french fries to a man. He looks just a little older than me. In boots and khaki shorts, he runs through the rain, hands covering his fries, to stand in the doorway with me. Although we talk lightly, I already know he will matter to me. He is from New Zealand. He asks where I camp at night. I don't have a tent. *Why would you set out from home without a tent?* I don't know. I didn't even know that I didn't have a tent until he mentioned it.

Acquiesence: He doesn't like my name. My name is "ethnic," but he doesn't say that is the problem. He only says, *It's an entirely forgettable name*, and he suggests another name for me. His name is Peter, and the name he suggests for me is Mary. A kind of disbelief drips like a drug into my blood. For a moment I feel very far away and ask myself, *If my name is forgettable how can any name be remembered?* Then I think of Peter, Paul and Mary and want to spray his face with spit, in a laugh. Only something in me has evaporated, and there is a new desert here, with fruit trees growing in the terraced hills, and fewer reasons to keep one name above any other. I swallow. *Okay*, I say, *if you want.*

The garden: It has stopped raining, and the valley has quickly regained its desert persona. We are like apostles looking for work after the crucifixion, going door to door seeing if anyone needs help. Finally an elderly couple, who live in a bungalow with a picture window that looks onto the lake, take us on as their gardeners. We tell them our names, and the man ponders them, *How biblical*. I know little about gardening and do a fair job of ripping up an entire asparagus patch before Peter intervenes. The more he smiles and calls me Mary, the better I learn to hate him. We sleep in a tent where I never let him touch me. It is not something I decide consciously, it's just that I don't like the shape of his feet or the feel of his hands. Evenings I go down to the orchards by myself. I sit in the man's pickup truck, play the radio and write poetry on scraps of paper.

Loosening up: Peter is jealous of my scraps of paper, he says, *Writing is your way of being selfish*. I won't show him my poems, but I play guitar for him. One night I am singing in a cherry orchard, when he decides he should be my manager. He tells me how it will be. *We'll get a VW van and travel up and down the coast*, me Mary, singing, he Peter, arranging the bookings. I say, *If you want*. When he is mowing the lawn the next morning I knock on the door of the man's house. *I just want you to know that my name isn't Mary*, and I tell him my real name. The man is puzzled. *Peter thought it was too forgettable*, I explain. Peter has already told him that we don't have sex. We are stranger than he thought, although, about the name, the man seems slightly relieved. *Your own name is much better*, he assures me. About the sex, his advice had been, Peter should loosen me up a little.

A tent: At the local cafe I find a notice for a Rainbow Festival, south of where we are. Something tells me that Celia might be there, angry but willing to makeup, stubborn but willing to change. We could finish the way and travel west together. The man is carrying his groceries up the stairs when I ask if he might have a tent that I could borrow for a week or so. I pretend I have already made the arrangements with Peter, to take a short trip by myself. It only takes an afternoon, and I'm deep in Dukobour territory on a pine soaked road, with a pup tent, my knapsack and guitar. Peter climbs down from his ladder a hundred miles away to find he has no way of finding his Mary.

Hell's Angels: Three arrowhead lakes slice through the mountains. They are shaped like a compass needle, tapered at the ends, pointing north to south. I take a small ferry across and walk the last miles down a road. At the end of it, there is folk-music, a big tent with vegetarian food, Sufi dancing, an astrologer and naked swimming in a mountain creek. Bearded men and their earth-mother old ladies have come to this unmarked place. I search for Celia, hopeful for her short hair among the patchouli scented women. Then I realize I have it wrong. In the makeshift parking lot, bikers have congregated. They rev their bikes the length of the day, turning the summer grass to muck. They are Hell's Angels, fallen angels, here, but not coming in. They brag and tussle. I go out to the parking lot and walk up and down the line of Harley's looking for Celia, loud and laughing among their women.

Love: By evening, I give up my search, go back inside and sit with one of the folkheroes. He is bearded, wearing a kind of free flowing moo-moo with sweat stains under his arms and beads around his neck. He is a poetry professor at a small American college and gets his summers off. He is like the kind of man my mother always thought I would marry. But he isn't happy. The seventies have bittered him, and the dawn of the eighties has brought only despair. *Nobody's hip anymore,* he tells me, *the sixties man, that was a time. Gasoline was 33 cents a gallon, acid was 25 cents a hit, and love was free.*

Eating soup: On Sunday night the festival folds the last of its tents. Up on a hill, I get a bowl of soup from a kitchen in a Volkswagen van. A small girl is rocking on her feet, repeating, almost chanting, *I hate soup, I hate soup, I hate soup.* A woman with big jewelry reaches out her hand, *I know you don't like soup and that's okay.* I am so struck by this that I stand still on my feet. I taste the soup. I can like soup or I don't have to like soup. It is my choice. A young man approaches me, says my name, but I don't know him. When he carefully takes a piece of paper from his wallet, I realize he is one of the French boys from the soft green hill. Celia gave him a note, in the chance he might find me. She knew she wouldn't find me herself. *Celia was tired of hitchhiking,* he tells me, *and took a bus straight to the coast.* She's been there for weeks. I put the note unread in the pocket of my jeans.

Reclaim: I share the night with my guitar, and when I sleep the guitar sleeps beside me. I'm not ready to sleep yet and sit with a single candle under the stars. I am trying to write down a few things, to keep a record of these days but the wind keeps putting its hand over the flame. *Okay, you want it dark? It will be dark,* and I let the wick be and set myself to try something that needs no light, automatic writing. I have never done this before and sceptically leave my hand resting on the page, free to go wherever. I try to clear my mind of thought. In a minute a nudge then my hand pushing across the page, doodling little circles, a compelling followed by a pause. Prepared to find nothing, I light the candle above the page only to see a word plainly written. *Reclaim.* Squelch the candle and put down the page. I feel the limit of something, a kind of line drawn at the edge of a life that marks the beginning of something larger. Around me the air feels too permeable, and who am I to think myself as big as the night? I roll the command through my fingers, but it is too vague: reclaim what? I would like to reclaim Celia, but she's gone west from me. I can't aim my hands towards any destination and blunder forward. Amnesia.

The rollerskaters: Celia's note I save until morning. *I hope you reach the ocean, and I hope you find love,* it says. At a small store with a payphone out front, I wait for the operator to put through my call. In the distance, a man and a woman approach, long legs wobbling on roller skates, young lovers. They come closer, become larger, and they have a puppy in tow, large paws, wrinkly face, huge pink tongue. By the time they reach the store, they are laughing so hard that they hold onto a tree for support. The puppy jumps and licks their hands. In that moment waiting for my line to connect, the rollerskaters frame a kind of ideal for me, of what men and women could be. I could aspire to that if I tried; I could try; and then a great relief to get my young brother on the line. No judgment. *Tell Dad I'll be home sooner than I said.* He asks if Celia will be with me, and I know how she fills his teenage summer with dreams. Celia: his older sister's friend, the vivacious one, always laughing. *No,* and I am angry too quickly and can't explain, *tell you later.* The empty tent I wrap like a deflated shell and send back to the man in a bus that goes one direction. The balance of me, also a kind of shell, sits on a green bench and waits for the bus back east to take me as far as it can go.

Travelling west: Celia went west without me, and a phone call is an inadequate way to describe a car trashing a guardrail, careening the cliffs into the sea, but this is how it is done. I came back east, hoping some sense of direction might come to me, thinking Celia might come home. Rousing myself from sleep, putting on my father's plaid housecoat, picking it up where he had thrown it on the floor, his breathing sounds coming from his room behind the kitchen, the stove broken again, the kitchen too cold and this impossible news of Celia. A set of words in which I hear the full sound of the car, the guardrail bursting and then a kind of silence at the sea's mouth. A swallow. *When did this happen?* I ask, not meaning the accident only, meaning all of this, the kitchen, the stove, my life hanging in a balance that is suddenly broken, when did all of this happen? Celia was travelling north on a highway when she missed a hairpin turn, and something terrible happened to her young body, her young body with the old heart in it. The phone rests in my cupped hands with the heavy weight of a gun. Geography fooled me. An axis shifted. Celia was travelling north, only to find west again.

♥ ♥ ♥

Want for Nothing

It's six p.m. on a Friday, and I'm finishing the last of a thousand calls I swear I've made this week. I should have known better about this job. "The glamorous world of advertising," the ad in the *Globe and Mail* had said. "Are you creative, good with people and looking for the challenge of your life?" That was two years ago, and I fell for it. Now I feel surgically attached to a telephone, wasting the best years of my life on cranky, tightfisted customers. Some glamorous world.

I'm trying to wrap up my last call — the one to the carpet cleaning company — when the highlight of my week, probably the highlight of my life, walks in dangling her car keys. I wave and gesture that I'll just be a second. She sidles up to me and writes a cute, little note: "Jingling of keys means get off the phone, leave the crummy office and come with me for a weekend of wild sex." She jingles.

Now, in my own defence, let me say that I am trying to get off the phone. I want to, really, but I have to be nice to the carpet-cleaning lady, and sometimes I just don't know how to say good-bye. I scribble back, "Justa sec." She looks at me in disbelief, then smirks and jangles her keys loudly into the receiver.

"Is that your other phone?" the carpet cleaner lady asks uncertainly.

"Phone?" The phones in our office beep rather than ring but she doesn't need to know that. "Yes. My goodness, my other line. Shall I call you first thing Monday?" and I try to go off, "Uh-huh, yes ... Okay, yes, right ... okay ... Is that so? ... yes, you too, bye now ... right ... uh-huh. Good-bye," I say finally and hang up.

"Well, that's done. Hi Cheryl, how's my baby?"

"Ready to go," she says.

"So am I. Here's our groceries for the weekend. Here's my suitcase of old clothes. Here's that terrible novel I borrowed from you last week. And here's what's left of me, ready to eat you up."

"All for me? I must have been a good girl," she smiles coyly. "You look beautiful. I want to kiss you."

"Wait until we get to the car, my love." I say, hurrying her towards the elevator. I'm dying to kiss her as we sprint across the underground parking lot at a quick pace. In the car we kiss a long time, until we've had enough to last the hour's drive north.

"You could have warned me about the book," I say.

"You didn't like it? But it's a classic."

"*Closeted Woman Kills Self in Anguish Over Lesbian Passion.* A bit tragic for my tastes."

"Sylvana it's literature. Hélène Robichaud is a brilliant writer. *Time* magazine called her a genius."

"If she really was a genius she could have racked her immense brain and come up with a happy ending."

"You're such a philistine sometimes. Hélène Robichaud is writing the true story of her friend Rebekah whose family ostracized her when they found out about her 'abnormal passions.' They wanted to institutionalize her for being a lesbian, so she drowned herself in a gesture of freedom. That was the only way she felt she could have control of her own destiny."

Freedom in well drownings. Glamour in advertising. Help me St. Teresa, I'm losing track here on earth.

"I know what you're saying, love, but it upsets me. The book is so claustrophobic. I wanted there to be a way out that wasn't jumping down a well."

"Sometimes there is, sometimes there isn't. You're forgetting how much has changed for lesbians in the past twenty years. And maybe Robichaud wrote a depressing story on purpose, so that the reader would know what it's like to be a lesbian in a repressed culture."

"Depressing people on purpose. Is that postmodern?"

Cheryl doesn't answer. She jams her foot on the accelerator and speeds the car up the parkway.

While she drives I lean back and admire — the view and her. Cheryl likes to drive. It gives her a feeling of smooth control in a rapidly changing world. Sometimes she likes to talk. She talks mostly about her ideas and about the details of her other lives, of which she has two. I rank third in her personal hierarchy and get to see her one day a week. Her live-in-lover Maia is in a constant battle for first place with Cheryl's work as a chiropractor.

After a while I notice Cheryl hasn't mentioned Maia yet. This means bad news. Casually I venture, "And how's Maia these days?"

Cheryl shoots me a look. A wince.

"It was a struggle to get this weekend that's for sure. She was sobbing on the couch when I left. It'll be a long time before we can do this again, I just want you to know."

Ingrid MacDonald

I can tell by the tone of her voice that she's being euphemistic. "A struggle" probably meant several hours of shouting and throwing things. Maia's not really big on Cheryl spending too much time with me, ever. I'm not much help either. If I call their house and Maia answers, I hang up. Maia always knows it's me too, which makes it worse. Several times Cheryl has patiently explained to me that it would be much better if I would just politely ask to speak to her. And I try, but I panic. I feel like such a kid. Every time I ask about Maia I half hope that Cheryl will say that Maia's taken a job on an archaeological dig and leaves for Yellowknife tomorrow.

At least I know better than to pursue this one. There have been times when I have pathetically begged Cheryl to leave Maia and devote herself to me. Each time, she flatly refused. Those conversations sit in my conscience as ugly disasters. Today I let the topic slide. Besides we got this weekend, which is what we wanted. What I wanted.

It is dusk as I give Cheryl the last few instructions to the farmhouse drive. Getting out of the car, I think how wonderful it would be if Cheryl and I were arriving here to live. I could leave the ad job, she could leave her chiropractic patients, we both could leave Maia far behind us in the city. We could be in love all day and everyday.

Wishing makes me silly with happiness. I rush over to Cheryl and grab her hand, "Well? Do you like our new home? Isn't it wonderful?" She hugs me, laughing. At least she likes my sense of humour. "I'll have to show you the orchard. It's so beautiful." I pull her around to the back of the house where the ground is bumpy with rust-coloured balls of fallen apples. The grass smells

124

musty and sweet. The late afternoon light turns her face a dark bronze. The sun turns the drying cornstalks to gold. The soil is black with humus where the tractors have turned it for fall. I am happy.

Inside I show her the wood piled by the stove, the pantry full of the season's yield: peaches, pickles, berries and from the farmer's market — olives, herring, rounds of cheese, vinegar, three kinds of oil, and long braids of garlic. I have brought fresh pasta, bread and a jar of homemade sauce. I want to assure her that she should want for nothing, that we'll be content for the rest of our lives, or at least for the weekend. I want her to have a sense of harvest, how there is plenty of everything.

This is such a departure for us. We're used to suffering the restraints of forbidden love. Hasty sex one day a week and days on end when we are unable to meet or speak. In the city, at my apartment, we've barely finished making love before she's rolling over and getting dressed again.

"What are you doing?" I ask, incredulous.

"It's nine-thirty. I said I'd be home."

"But how can you walk?"

Then I'm courteous in a way that I know hurts her, showing her the door, offering her a cold cheek to kiss goodbye.

I offer to make some food, though I know it is not food she wants. She smiles and says, "Not just now." She is still smiling as I take her hand and lead her upstairs.

Upstairs there is a room with a bed. Decorated by my mother, I have left it untouched since my girlhood. I can be so sentimental, it pains me at times. On the wall are pictures of animals (cat family) and of the Blessed Virgin Mary (holy family). On the bed are pillows in hand-crocheted coverings and dolls with glass eyes.

In my tailored suit, I seem large and unlikely in such a nostalgic room. But I have chosen not to change the decoration. I rarely visit my mother and often miss her. She doesn't live that far away from the farmhouse, and sometimes I hope she'll drop by.

Cheryl laughs. "This is pretty lady-like for a butch like you, Miss Lacuna."

"Too bad you love it, Miss Shablynski."

"You're right I do," she says crossing the room. She kisses me and starts to undo the buttons on my shirt.

When we begin I always want to make love to her first. I'm electric with hunger, afraid I won't be able to fill the emptiness inside me. Under her layers of clothes, I feel her heavy breasts. I stroke them, feeling for the hardening nipples as she makes wonderful noises. Her kisses become harder. My hands move up and down the length of her back, around the sides of her body, returning again and again to her wonderful breasts. I bring my lips to hers and softly, softly smooth her forehead and cheeks, feeling for the small hairs that cover her skin. Then I hold the back of her head with my palms and kiss her long and hard.

She is pulling on my clothes now, slipping my jacket to the floor. When she goes for my belt buckle I move her hands away and help her off with her clothes instead. Then I throw open the bed clothes and pause for the slightest second to arrange the pillows for her head. She leans back. I tease her with the fabric of my pants against her skin. She grabs for my nipples through my unbuttoned shirt, sucking one while pulling the other with a furled hand. Her eyes are closed, and I feel intense emotion coming off her in waves, like a kind of heat. I hold her tight, kissing her.

Reaching down I find the handful of warm wetness and the

sopping lips of her cunt. My hand caresses the folds, holding off for just a moment to let her pleasure rise before I safely, safely slip on a translucent rubber glove and dab a drop of jelly on my fingers. As I go in with two fingers, she moans and breathes deeply. She makes these high, effluent, whinnying sounds. I kiss her making my mouth hollow and round; she pushes her tongue in and out. I am watching her intently as I move more fingers into her cunt. I ease with careful persistence. Down the warm glove of her vagina, until all my five fingers are curled tightly into her. I feel the back of my hand against the base of her cunt, my fingertips arch to feel her smooth front wall, the back of my fingers feel the soft knob of her cervix. I have slipped one arm under her neck to hold her firmly, lovingly, while I rock my hand inside her, drawing it in and out to the rhythm of her breath. I can tell by her voice that she is faraway and given over to the pleasure in her body. The slightest movement sends her deep into pleasure. I fuck her this gently until she lets me know she has had enough.

I take my hand out — slowly unwinding it. Her clit needs only to be breathed on, and she's alive with feeling, inhaling and shuddering as I stroke her, brushing my hand across her clit, now large and pink and hard in her glistening lips. Holding her, watching her, I am overwhelmed with awe. Listening to her tight, rapid breaths, I touch her clit with long strokes. She gasps and folds her legs across my hand to hold it, then she gasps again and lets go. For a long time after that I hold her, caressing her face until we fall asleep.

The sound of a car coming up the driveway wakes us. We are both naked under the covers, and the morning is dazzling and

Ingrid MacDonald

bright. Sun streams through the lace-covered windows. A car horn honks.

"Who could that be?" I wonder, putting on a robe and moving to the window, shielding my eyes from the brightness. "Oh my god," I say looking out and recognizing the woman getting out of the car below. I open the window.

Cheryl is suddenly awake. "Who is it?"

"It's my mother."

"Your mother?" She looks as the clock. "Does she always visit at eight o'clock on Saturday mornings?"

"Hardly ever."

"What should I do? Should I hide?"

"Don't worry, she'll love you. I told her all about you on the phone."

"You told her about me?" Cheryl is aghast. "What did you tell her? That you're sleeping with a lapsed-Catholic adulteress? Oh my god Jan, I can't believe it. I'm naked in your bed, and your mother is in the driveway."

"Will you relax?" I lean out the window, "Hi Mom. Did you bring eggs? That's so thoughtful of you." My mother is wearing a beige linen dress that she made herself. She's all radiant, what with the sun and the linen and the shining mists.

She shouts up, waving, "Hi Jan. How's my little girl? Being good? Your father was asking last night how you were. I thought I'd come over to see if you were around."

"I'm great Ma. You look beautiful, I gotta tell ya."

"Have you got someone up there with you Jan?"

I grin sheepishly, "Yaah."

"I can always tell when you are with someone. Is it the one with the other girlfriend?"

"That's the one. Her name is Cheryl, I told you before."

128

"Oh yes, Cheryl. Tell her to come to the window. I want to talk to her."

I turn back to the room. Cheryl is sitting with the sheet wrapped over her breasts. She looks like she has been trying not to breathe. "Cher, my mom wants to talk to you."

"To me? What does she want to talk to me about? Tell her I'm not dressed yet. Tell her I'm asleep."

"I can't say that, it would hurt her feelings. Just talk to her a bit."

"Okay," she groans and reluctantly shuffles to the window in her bed sheet. "Hello Mrs. Lacuna, a beautiful morning today."

"Hello there Cheryl. Now listen, do you love my daughter?"

Speechless, Cheryl turns back to me, "What should I say?" Her eyes are wild with surprise.

"Just answer her. Tell her the truth."

"Oh that." Cheryl wrinkles her nose for a second and sticks her head out the window again. Clutching her sheet she says, "Yes, I do love your daughter. Very much so, Mrs. Lacuna."

"But you've got trouble with the other girlfriend all the time, yes?"

"Well not all the time. It's not always easy if that's what you mean."

"And Jan, she makes you happy, doesn't she? I mean she's a nice girl, she works hard, she has that glamorous job in advertising, and she makes you feel good. Yes?"

"Well, yes. I love being with her when I can."

"So why don't you leave that other woman and be with Jan? She gets so upset when you're not around. Sometimes she calls me and oh, she cries and cries."

"I've never thought of it that way before, Mrs. Lacuna. You mean I should just leave Maia and be Jan's lover and forget this once a week business?"

"That's right."

"Okay, well now that we've talked about it, that seems like a good idea. I'll do that then. Just let me tell Jan."

When Cheryl turned back to the room I was asleep. She said, "Jan. Jan. Honey."

I woke up to the dazzling white sun streaming through the lace behind Cheryl's back. "Jan, there's a woman in the driveway."

I was groggy. "What does she look like?"

"I don't know. Older. Wearing a flowered dress and an apron."

I put on my robe and looked out but it was only Mrs. Grodin bringing the milk. I leaned out, "Thank you Mrs. Grodin, just leave it on the steps, and I'll pay you Sunday." She nodded and the bottles clinked down. I stood watching out the window as she drove away, feeling Cheryl's arms around me from behind, wanting no more than what we had, and lacking nothing. I could feel her breasts and her belly, their warmth against the silk of my robe.

❖ ❖ ❖

The Second Language

My mother has bought me my first book, and we read it everyday. Our Evelyn gives me chocolate for a special treat. Evelyn is from the home country, which is somehow not here, not either our home or this country. It is faraway, where the boxes of clothes and sweets come from at Christmas. From the corner of the kitchen I watch Evelyn pour tea. The words sit on the page of my new book, and my mother lifts them off for me. I don't want to memorize their pictures. I want to memorize their sound. A tea pot is shaped the way Evelyn is. I play with my brother's airplane. Evelyn hands a cup and saucer to my mother and reads a happy story on my mother's face. I ask Evelyn if I could have a cup and saucer too. My mother and Evelyn laugh. Evelyn gives me another chocolate. Sweet thick chocolate paste fills up my mouth. Evelyn cuts a cake for my mother, a high round cake with a drizzle icing on top.

Sister Superior has a large black desk where she rests her hands, the good hand and the one that's a puffy claw, where the paper cutter came down. A scar on the back of her hand like a zipper. She writes my name into the long book with the names of all the children. Careful slanted writing, small and spiky. I didn't know I had two names. Sister asks Mummy about the spelling and they disagree. Then Sister crosses a word out and writes it again. Mummy says Sister reminds her of when she was a little girl. I can't imagine how something large was once small, like my mother's hands which are so much larger than mine. The i's and e's in my name are mixed up in Sister's long book, as the door is opened for Mummy to go through, and she's given something up, me maybe, but more than me. The way we spell my name, she has given up and the hall feels cold and large. It was the only word I knew how to spell. Sister holds me beside her skirt and says, 'Say goodbye now. Be strong child,' but it isn't being strong to be this weak and Mummy has already given away the i and the e.

Sister takes me to a room where the blackboard holds two more words. A lady in a green dress stands in front of them and points with a stick. 'I am Mrs. Patrick,' she says. Miss-Sis Pah-Trick. Mrs. Patrick.

Mrs. Patrick looks at me, seeing all of me at once and from the outside. I can only see my hands and my legs. When Evelyn hugs me to her belly, all of me disappears into her apron dusty with icing sugar. She rolls me like a crêpe. My mother is not here, not either in Mrs. Patrick's classroom with the chalkboard or looking out the kitchen window with Evelyn. My mother gave her a list of things for the store, which Evelyn reads. First we have to find her glasses.

Mrs. Patrick has me sit still while she puts letters in front of me. One letter at a time, the exercise is useless. The letter A is ugly. It is not a whole word. Mrs. Patrick says apple. Ah-Pull. A is only a broken off bit of the word. No man can keep water in a broken cup, Mummy says, you must ask Jesus to help you be a beautiful vessel. There is a picture of Jesus on the wall, children at his feet. Mrs. Patrick looks at me from the outside. She says, 'Go and wash your hands,' 'They aren't dirty,' I hold them up. 'Do as you are told.'

At snack time, Louise eats a banana and the others make fun of her. Every day the same brown banana comes out of her plastic box. She eats it dutifully and then we practise writing the alphabet, a code she is giving us in broken fragments one letter at a time. The blue pencil writes F's on the lines in the scribbler. I like the capital F, tall and straight with flags coming off it. I make a perfect page of perfect F's. The big blue pencil marches across the blue lines. I take them to Mrs. Patrick where she sits in the middle of the room. She nods at the F's and then her eye drifts to the other page. A page of yesterday's fives that my hand has smeared. Smudges from the blue pencil. 'What's this? A terrible mess. What are you showing me this mess for?' After that the number five and the letter F get stuck. When I go to write a word, I put a number in instead. a5raid. 5ather. 5all.

Sister comes in her long skirts and says we can ask Jesus for anything. She is wearing an apron and carrying a basket with branches from a bush she pruned. I ask Jesus for the miracle of the ascension. Every night I dream of my miracle and see Mrs. Patrick taken into heaven. Over the school playground she floats huge, waving goodbye to the children below. She doesn't know it was my special prayer that put her there. She thinks she earned it with her hard lived life. 'Goodbye my little ones,' she says. Every morning she finds her way back to school with her brown shoes on. The lord gives and the lord takes away, my mother says.

On Fridays in the afternoon, we are allowed to draw pictures. The other children draw stick figures. Their crayons skid across

Ingrid MacDonald

the newsprint in their clumsy hands. They draw clouds and gardens and trees shaped like green balls. Louise draws a sun with rays like spider legs and eats a brown banana. When we play Simon Says, she throws up. The janitor brings a grey mop. There is a paper on the kitchen table. I ask Evelyn what does it mean. 'Find me my glasses,' she says. Mummy has gone to the cinema for the afternoon, it says. The house feels lonely without her even though we have Evelyn and her sugary apron. Evelyn is busy cooking, she doesn't see Mrs. Patrick outside levitating above the treeline in her stocking feet. It is fall and the trees show their bones, tall inside-out umbrellas at the edge of the sky. 'Evelyn, can we close the curtains?' I ask.

Mrs. Patrick closes the curtains and shows a movie in the dark. Louise has been away for a week. 'One of us is sick and we will have to pray,' she says, looking at Louise's empty desk but not saying her name. We must all wash our hands carefully. Jesus washes the lepers and lets an old woman touch the bottom of his robe. Mrs. Patrick tells us to draw pictures of what we saw in the movie. I draw poor Louise on a stretcher, being lowered through the roof. Jesus has his arms stretched up in surprise, in welcome. The other children draw clouds and trees and stick figures, green balls and yellow suns. Jesus says comforting things to Louise.

Mrs. Patrick shouts. 'You drew this?' She is strangely happy. She holds the picture in both her hands, and holds it up where it is glorious and beautiful. A real picture with the house looking like a real house and the faces looking real. And Jesus especially real, with compassion in his eyes. Then she says, 'But what's this?' Jabs her finger in the sky behind the house. 'It's an airplane.' A floating airplane that looks like a lady with brown shoes on. 'There were no airplanes when Jesus lived.' 'Yes there were.' 'Never mind your fresh talk.' She rips the page in four pieces. 'Blasphemy,' she says.

(II)

Mummy is fighting with Evelyn so Evelyn went in someone else's car. 'Let her,' my mother says. My brother left his communion suit on even though he's allowed to eat now, and he'll go in the races. He's kept his mouth clean for Jesus since yesterday. Mummy fixes her lipstick in the rearview mirror and says, 'I hope she knows what she's doing.' She pats her cheeks with a round powder pad. My mother pucks her lips with a smack. 'She's so slovenly,' she says. My brother puts his hands over his ears. Slovenly, so lovenly, slow lovingly, I think. 'What's slovenly mean?' I ask. She looks at me in the mirror, raising her eyebrows like I should know not to ask some questions. 'Oh it's just the way Evelyn is.' 'But what does it mean?' 'It means she doesn't wash afterwards.' 'After what?' 'After anything,' she says, 'and don't you go running to her and tell her I say so.'

I have a new teacher in school this year, Miss Lord. 'Is that your real name?' one of the kids asks. Mrs. Patrick would have made you stand in the corner for asking something as rude as that. Miss Lord has square glasses and shoulder-length hair and is soft and square as a mattress. She kind of laughs at things we say. 'Not only is my name Miss Lord,' she says, 'but my first name is Hope: my hope is in the Lord.' This is the first time I've known the first name and last name of an adult.

The fathers are wearing wool pants and leather shoes and carry the platters of cooked chicken and bread out of the cars. Sister has brought a basket of sweets for the communion children. She kisses them one by one and puts a candy in their hands. The priest puts up the strings for the races and carries the badges in a paper bag. I want to go in the race for younger children, but I want Evelyn to watch me, and I ask where she is. My mother points to a stand of trees. She pretends she's holding a smelly hanky and wrinkles her nose. 'Over there somewhere,' she says. I look across the field towards the trees. The grass is alive with flinging things, grasshoppers with green speckly legs and butterflies that land lightly.

Sometimes I know how to read and sometimes I don't. Miss Lord sits a group of us in a semi-circle, on little chairs with our books in our laps. The bigger children are breaking through the strings at the finish line. Around the bend of the trees there is a small creek. The shouting voices, cheers and clapping fall away in the trees. We have to read outloud from our books and I don't know if I am going to be able to do it. She calls my name for my turn, and I feel a blankness come over me, but then I hear my voice reading the words from the page, each sentence is like a ribbon that pours out, a whole paragraph pours as the floor tilts slightly and I feel a flying feeling. 'Very good,' Miss Lord says. She is smiling. 'That was excellent.' I feel a soft landing feeling and my cheeks burn. I look at my book's page, where I hide my eyes.

Trees sound like breathing. A bee lumbers in the grass, and I find Evelyn. She has taken her shoes off and lies on her belly, in her red flowered dress, on her blanket, reading. The races seem faraway, elsewhere, and this part near the trees is so quiet and warm. 'Is this near the home country?' I ask. 'Where?' she says. 'This place, this park.' She shakes her head and smiles. 'No,' she says. 'The home country is quite far.' 'As faraway as the races?' 'Much further,' she says.

The Second Language

I want to sit with her but it's too much, and I don't want to sit with her because it isn't enough. I look in Evelyn's eyes and our blood talks. She's so lovely. It feels like blood talking when I look at her, and my arms and legs tingle, and I don't know what I want and worry about what might happen to me if I touched her the way my blood talking wants to touch. The trees and the flinging things and the children and Miss Lord and the books we read at school make an envelope, and inside the envelope I have hidden a page where I write my secret words for Evelyn. It's folded up there, and I wonder if Evelyn can see it when she looks in my eyes.

Maybe she sees through there to my secret page because Evelyn looks at me curiously, puts her book down and says, 'Come here child,' and I kneel in front of her, and she lays me down and pats my hair with her warm hands. She strokes my cheeks with her fingers and draws the outline of my mouth with her fingertips. I take one of her fingers with my lips and pull it into my mouth, and suck. She pulls her finger gently out and undoes the front of her blouse and offers me one of her large nipples.

I am drifting upwards like a balloon, held tight by the knot of Evelyn's pink nipple, and everything in me is string, a single limp string tied at my mouth to Evelyn's round breast. Her chest rises and falls and I rest there, buoyant, tethered, sucking.

When I look up again she is reading. 'No,' she says. 'The home country is quite far.' I push myself close to her belly and button her blouse up for her, so she doesn't have to move. I don't want her to move. The words on the page are small and long and hard to read, without any pictures. I wonder why people read books without pictures, how people can read words that are so small.

Around me I see butterflies landing, their wings pause and wave. I try to imagine how something large was once small. In the sun, wings are paperthin velvet where wheels and beads and lace in purple and brown and gold have been painted. Evelyn's skin is warm from the sun. Evelyn's hand absently strokes my hair, her eyes following the words on their page, her fingers turning the pages of the book. I look at her averted face and feel my blood talking but this time it's different. I see the small words in her books and I want to know them. I raise my hand to Evelyn's cheek and whisper, 'Teach me to read.'

(III)

The three o'clock bell has gone and children stream out the side doors, for a moment everything is red and blue stripes bouncing. I see my mother waiting in the car way over at the other side. Away from the other mothers. The other mothers bring cookies wrapped in paper napkins. They hold them out gingerly, as if they want a bird to land on their hands. Some mothers come every day and wait but my mother doesn't. When she does come, she parks at the end of the playground and waits silently. She doesn't honk or call. Her freckled brown arm is on the rolled-down window, and she's day dreaming out the window, like it was a movie screen. Ours is a rusty red Ford with pointy parts over the lights, the colour of the playground swings in September. I'm not sure if I should disturb her, but she knows I'm there without looking. 'Get in if you like,' she says, and she means it just like that. I can get in or I don't have to. I get in.

She's been shopping, and I don't know where my brother has gotten to. I put my reader-book on my lap. We are reading about the Canadian soldiers and Canadian airplanes during the war. My brown sweater feels warm against the burgundy velvet seats. My mother looks out the window, in the wrong direction, faraway. Then she adjusts the rear-view mirror. 'He's a walker,' she says about my brother. 'It's only direct up the hill.'

She says 'direct.' In school we have to say 'directly' or its not right. Some words make me suspicious. The more I learn in school about words the more I think she and I speak something different. Words come in categories. When I spell words wrong, I lose marks. My mother's voice is soft and brown and it penetrates me. When we speak, all the nouns and adjectives and verbs blend into one thing. It can't be written down. Her voice and the words in our readers and on the blackboards and in our scribblers just don't seem the same to me.

She reaches into the backseat, into a bushel basket of ripe field tomatoes. I ask, 'What language are we?' 'Canadian,' she says. 'Then what language are you?' I ask. She chooses two tomatoes very carefully, concentrating and doesn't answer right away. 'Canadian too,' she says a little angrily. 'Who wants to know?' 'Just me,' I say.

'I was at Rudi's,' she says, handing me a tomato. 'Here, go have one.' It is as big as both my hands. I see Sister go by in her long skirts with two long sticks of bread in her wicker basket. I bite into the tomato, and my mother hands me her hanky and says, 'We got a letter from Evelyn today. She sends her love.' I imagine Evelyn in the home country with a bowl of hot chocolate in her lap. I'm not sure where she is exactly, but there are mountains there and wardrobes of clothes and kitchens of sweet things. My mouth fills with sweet red tomato and stings at the edges.

The playground is empty and my brother hasn't come.

Ingrid MacDonald

There's only the hopscotch squares and me and my mother, direct under the sun. A jet dangles a single letter I in the blue sky that drifts and dissolves. I look at my mother as she wipes her lips with her hands and licks the red juice from her fingers. I'd like to know what her real name is, other than Mummy. One day, when I have her attention, I'll have to ask.

Ingrid MacDonald was born in southern Ontario in 1960 of a German mother and Cape Breton father. She has contributed extensively to feminist and lesbian and gay media in Toronto as a writer and broadcaster. Her short story "Travelling West" was a winner in the 1990 *Prism International* fiction contest. Ingrid has adapted "The Catherine Trilogy" for the stage in a play called *The Catherine Wheel*. A graduate of the University of Toronto in religion and literary studies, Ingrid lives in Toronto and writes full-time. *Catherine, Catherine* is her first collection of short stories.